Roommates

Briton Frost

Published by Briton Frost, 2019.

This is a work of fiction. Similarities to real people, places, or events are entirely coincidental.

ROOMMATES

First edition. February 5, 2019.

Copyright © 2019 Briton Frost.

ISBN: 978-1795073042

Written by Briton Frost.

CHAPTER ONE

MATTHEW

My roommate is giving me a hard-on.

He's breezing in and out of the room now because he's getting ready to go out on a date. It's just as well. He smells too damn good, and one of these times he passes by me on the couch, I'm liable to reach out and pull him down to me. Mold my hands around that ass. Kiss those lips that haunt my dreams all night long and tempt my control in the daylight hours. And his Adam's apple. I don't think I ever paid much attention to a guy's neck before, but I am obsessed with Beckett's throat.

He doesn't know what he's doing to me. How he's awakened the…I guess you'd call it…alpha beast…inside me. Hell, if he knew about the things I want to do to him, he'd pack a bag and run.

But that's just it. Where would he go?

My only saving grace right now is that he thinks I'm straight. And that's for the best. It helps me keep my hands off him. Most alphas and omegas are gay, but not all. But an alpha can only impregnate an omega, and an omega can only conceive with alpha seed.

I've spent the last four years taking care of Beckett from afar, but he doesn't know it. He doesn't know that the renewable, annual scholarship that paid his tuition, room, and board all through college was funded by me. He doesn't know the car he "won" is a gift from me, either.

And the condo? It's mine, too. That he knows. He was supposed to be housesitting for me while I was out on the oil rig. But until I'm done with physical therapy and my foot injury is healed enough to go back to work, my ass is planted on this couch during the day and the guest room at night.

Yeah, I sleep in the guest room of my own house.

I only bought this condo so Beckett would have a safe place to stay. I had to buy furniture to make it look even a little lived in. I used to just have a small shitty apartment and storage for what little stuff I owned. I spend most of my life on the oil rig where I work. When I have time off, I usually travel on my Harley or park my ass on a Mexican beach. Away from people.

So sure, I told him to take the master suite when I asked him to move in. I made sure it had luxury everything because I wanted him to live here a long time so I could easily keep an eye on him.

I'm not a stalker or anything.

I'm just a man of my word. I made a promise to his brother.

My best friend, Beckett's older brother Cameron, was in a bad car wreck four years ago. There was nothing I wouldn't do for my buddy, he was more like my brother than a friend, so when he made me promise to look out for his baby brother, I vowed to him I would.

And then he died.

This is not what Cam meant when he asked me to take care of Beckett. The way I imagine defiling him over and over again. Beckett's too sweet for a guy like me. Too pure.

He was raised to be a good boy. From a good family. Cam and Beckett's parents are respectable people, but not rich people. Cam had been helping them with bills and had been planning on helping with college for his baby brother. His dying left them in a bad place, emotionally and financially. I'm not rich or anything, but I make damn good money, and I don't spend much of it. So, I played like Santa's fucking elf and took care of shit.

But Cam's baby brother isn't a baby anymore. Something I wasn't prepared for when I moved back into the condo for the summer.

He's fucking hot and he's not even my type. His body has got my hands itching. I want to map every inch of him with my tongue. He's not as big as the guys I usually get hot for. I like the gym rats and the bears, mostly because I don't have to worry about hurting them. But Beckett's plump ass is juicy and hard to ignore. It makes me want to grab him, hold him down, and fuck him hard.

I want him as mine.

He's too young. Too innocent. And he wants the kind of life that includes a picket fence and family portraits on Instagram. I'm not that guy. I'm the guy who could fuck him, and fuck him well. But that's it.

I'd wreck him, though. I'm too brutal. Too rough. Too big. Everywhere.

So, I haven't told him that I'm gay, too. He just assumes I'm straight because his brother was my best friend, and Cameron was a fucking pussy magnet. Seriously, women used to just drop their panties around him. If I had been into chicks, we would have been a lot more trouble together.

But I'm partial to dick. Really, really partial.

"Matthew? How's your foot?" He's standing adjusting his jacket sleeves. Because he's ready to go. On his date. With a guy who isn't me.

I want to punch a fucking wall, but I've got no right.

"It's fine." My foot hardly ever bothers me, but the doctors say my threshold for pain is high, too high, so I need to be even more careful. I don't like feeling like a wuss and doing nothing when I should be working, but if I reinjure it because I don't feel the pain, I could end up permanently unable to go back to my job.

"Did you take your pill?" He's holding my prescription, rattling the pills in the bottle. I hate those things.

"I don't need one."

"Matthew, you know what the doctor said."

I give him what I hope is a reassuring smile. "I'm not in any pain. Now go. Text me when you get there so I know you're safe."

"Okay, Daddy." He sticks his tongue out at me.

Fuck me. I know he means it in a funny, sarcastic way. But all I can think of is him calling me "Daddy" when I'm pumping my cock into him. And that tongue he stuck out, the dreams I've been having about that tongue…

I need to get back to work on the rig. There is no way I can survive the summer in close quarters with him and keep our relationship platonic. He thinks of me like some kind of foster big brother. I'm supposed to think of him like a sweet, baby brother.

But I don't. I used to. But I don't anymore. Not since I saw him for the first time in the flesh last month.

Back when Cam was alive, I saw his pictures of Beckett, and they never did anything for me. He was cute then. Awkward, with too long of limbs and a mouth full of metal. A teenager. After Cam died, I saw Beckett once at the funeral, and again...he was just a cute kid. I kept in contact with his parents, and he and I texted sometimes or emailed. But I hadn't seen him since. I didn't know.

He's a man now. A beautiful one. But a sweet one. Somehow naïve despite the world we live in. Cam would expect me to honor that. Take care of that innocence.

Not fuck it right out of him. Like I want to.

And so, instead of hooking my arm around his waist and bringing all that juicy, plump ass into my lap, I send him off on a date with someone else. I don't get to be territorial.

But I swear to God I want to kill this Trent or whatever the fuck his name is that's taking him to a ballgame. I'm pretty sure Beckett doesn't even like baseball. I doubt Trent cares.

"Dinner is in the fridge. You just need to nuke it to warm it up." He does that. Every night now.

"You don't have to cook for me. I'm not an invalid. I can cook my own food." My words come out short and grumpy. Which is how I feel, but he doesn't deserve that.

"I know I don't have to. I like taking care of you. Besides, it's the least I can do when you let me live here rent free."

"You're doing me a favor. I don't like leaving this place empty." I shake my head. "Sorry I snapped at you. You know I love your cooking, right?" Because I do. It's like...this is going to sound stupid...but it's like I can feel how much he cares in each bite.

He smiles at me and it's ...fuck me...it's adorable. There, I said it. I find him adorable.

Never in my life has that been something I've gone for. I like big, hard guys. Guys I won't crush. Guys who don't want to take care of me or even hang out when we're through fucking.

But I have a crush. On an adorable, innocent, really nice guy.

As soon as he leaves, I'm going to have to rub one out because my balls are fucking full.

He gets to the door when his phone dings, and he looks down at the message. His face falls. His lips press into a tight line, and his hand starts to shake. I'm across the room before I realize I've gotten up. "What's wrong?"

He shakes his head. "Nothing."

Fuck that shit. I take his phone, hold his wrist when he tries to get it back. I read the message.

Decided I don't want you to get the wrong idea. Just want to be friends. It's not you, it's me. Best we skip game. Taking my brother instead.

That little fuck.

"May I have my phone, please?" His voice is strained.

"He's a punk."

"Whatever." He takes his phone back. "I'm just going to go lay down for a while. I have a headache."

I haven't let go of his wrist. "Don't do that. Don't let the punk who wasn't good enough for you make you feel bad. He's an asshole."

"You don't even know him."

"Any guy that cancels at the last minute by text is an asshole. I promise. You deserve better."

Shit. He looks so sad. I don't know how to handle sad. I can barely handle his smiles. They make me try to think of shit to keep him happy. But sad, man, I will rip the arms off the bastard punk who dumped him if it stops Beckett from being unhappy. I'll do whatever the fuck he needs to never see this expression again.

"I'm not really sure I deserve better anymore. It's starting to feel like I don't deserve anyone at all." He frowns at me while looking at my foot and then over to the couch. "You left your cane over there."

He brings it to me, and I grab an arm around his middle and make him sit on the couch with me. "Tell me what's going on."

Beckett covers his face with his hands. "I don't want to."

"Becks," I growl. I can't fix it if I don't know. Did he really like that guy? Should I go drag his ass back here?

"I need some kind of intervention. I'm so stupid."

"Now you're pissing me off. There's nothing about you that is stupid. What's going on?"

"There *is* something wrong with me, and I really don't think you're the person I can talk to about it."

That kind of hurts, and I don't know why.

"You can tell me anything."

"Not this."

I'm holding in a growl. Actually, it's more like a primal howl. He's holding back from me. Hiding something from me. It should be his own damn business; he owes me nothing at all. But tell that to the caveman inside who thinks he belongs to us.

"You can tell me anything. I'll always help you. You know that."

"I don't think you want to help me with this. *Nobody*, it seems, wants to help me with this."

I'm trying to be patient. Really, I am. "Have I ever let you down?"

He looks at me, his eyes shining. "No. You're the best man I know, Matthew."

"Well, that's pushing it." I clench my hand to keep from reaching for his hair because I want to run my hand through it. "Just tell me what the problem is. I'll make it better. You know I will. I can fix damn near anything."

"The problem is...oh God, I can't believe I'm telling you this. The problem is that I'm a virgin."

CHAPTER TWO

BECKETT

I want to reach out and pull the words back into my mouth. But they are out there now, and Matthew looks like I just slapped him across the face.

"You're a virgin?"

Like, is this the worst thing in the world or something? I mean, it's a little annoying to me, but why is this some big issue for him? "Never mind. It's not a big deal."

"Were you going to give it to him?"

Now I feel like the one who got slapped. *It*? Crass much? "Maybe I was. It doesn't matter now, does it? Trent didn't want it. *Nobody* wants it." And I am making this hole so much deeper than it needs to be. But hey...I can crawl into it and hide now.

"Why?"

"Why what?"

He leans back against the cushion. "Why are you still a virgin? Why were you going to give it to him? Why nobody else? I don't know. I'm trying to figure out what's going on."

I want to tell him it's none of his business. But I guess I made it his business when I told him. "In high school, after I tested positive for the omega gene, I wasn't sure I was gay. Well, I probably was sure, but I wasn't ready to admit it to myself. Cam was my idol and I wanted to be cis-het just like him. In college, I don't know...I was still sad about my brother dying, and then I was just too busy to worry much about guys or getting pregnant. So, I knew I was attracted to them, but I never got up close and personal with anyone. Now, I've waited this long, so it feels like I should at least be serious about someone before I have sex with them. At the very least, third date material. Except, I can't seem to get a second date. Which means no third date." I cover my face again. This is too much. Matthew does not need to know this.

He pulls my hands back down. He's shifted so he's hovering a little so he can keep my wrists at my side. "Why?"

"Why do I want to wait for a third date to have sex? I don't know. I guess I'm old fashioned. I'm not really a Grindr kind of guy. I realize many gay dudes are freer with sex than I am but—"

"No, why don't you go on second and third dates?"

I shrug. I don't know how to explain it. If I did, I wouldn't have this problem. "I get asked out on first dates, and I even do the asking sometimes, so some guys find me attractive, I guess. But everything just fizzles out on the dates. Sometimes I know it's not going anywhere, so I don't expect a call, or I ask them not to call. But lately, I've been willing to at least *try* date number two...but it never surfaces. Maybe they can smell my desperation." I look into his dark eyes. They are so intense. So focused on me. I have to swallow hard. My throat feels tight. "Do I smell desperate to you?"

I tilt my head to look at him. His face is close. I can feel the heat of his skin. His breath on me. The world pauses for a second until he blinks like he's waking up. "You smell like cookies to me. And cinnamon rolls."

I inhale sharply. His words kiss something inside me, and my belly tightens.

"Cookies?"

"Yeah. And cinnamon rolls. You smell good."

I have to laugh a little. He doesn't pay compliments like most people. But you never have to wonder if he means what he says. There's nothing artificial in his words. Ever. If he says I smell like cookies, that means he likes how I smell because I've seen how much he likes cookies. I'll have to bake cinnamon rolls this weekend and see how he feels about them.

"I don't know what I'd do without you, Matthew." Sometimes I wonder what I'd do *with* him, if given the chance. Matthew is like every dream, every fantasy, I've ever had rolled into one extra-large, extra-handsome package. Nothing about him is soft or sweet at first glance. He's big, beastly really. Every muscle comes from hard work. But the sweetness is there, under the rough exterior.

He thinks of me like a little brother, though. And he's straight. I just worship him from afar. If I can't get a guy like Trent, there's no way I could get a guy like Matthew, even if we played on the same team. I don't know the kind of women he dates, but I can guess. Not the kind who teach kindergarten who've never seen a penis up close that wasn't on a porn site.

So, yeah, getting distracted now.

"Well, there are worse things to smell like than cookies," I say. "But then I still don't know what's wrong with me. All I've ever really wanted was a family of my own, and maybe that's the problem. Even though I don't wear a sign that says, "I want to get married and have babies with you," that's what they sense. But I don't want to just jump into a committed relationship any more than they do. I just want to see where things could go." I pat his knee. "I really am going to go lay down for a while. I think I need comfy clothes and Mr. Darcy."

A man in a wet, white shirt will go a long way in fixing this day.

"Who is Mr. Darcy?"

I roll my eyes. I maybe minored in English Lit, but even if I hadn't, I'd love Colin Firth in a wet shirt. "*Pride and Prejudice*." He looks at me blankly. "Jane Austen. None of that rings a bell?"

He shakes his head. "Nope." He stops me from getting up. Just thrusts one well-muscled arm out. "There is nothing wrong with you."

"I just need to be alone. I'll be fine." Is it wrong that something about his forceful hold makes me hard? It's...hot. Maybe my alone time will include some...me time.

"Bring the movie out here. We'll watch it together." I start laughing. "What?" he asks. He looks so serious. And seriously confused.

"I don't think it's your kind of flick."

"Bring it out."

"You'll hate it."

"If you like it, I'll like it."

"No, you won't. But okay. I'm feeling just mean enough to make you sit through it."

CHAPTER THREE

MATTHEW

I fucking hate it.

Everything about this movie is awful. It's boring. I can't understand what they're saying. Nobody bangs anybody, and there are no car chases.

But Beckett is asleep with his head resting on my shoulder, and I'm not moving.

Maybe ever.

Everything about him is pleasing to me. I want to explore every inch of him with my hands and my mouth. See if he tastes as sugary as he smells.

I got it bad man.

And he's cherry.

Shit.

I don't know what to do with that information. I know what I want to do with it. He thinks it's an anchor, but to me it's a beacon. A homing signal. I want to be his first...and his last. That's the scary part.

He deserves a guy who'll marry the shit out of him and keep his belly full of babies. Take care of him. Be his partner. Me? I don't know how to do that. There's a reason I work on a fucking oil rig in the middle of the goddamned ocean, man. I never wanted hearth and home and whatever goes along with it. I like knowing my life can fit in a rucksack if I need it to. I don't want a husband or kids or a house.

But I wish I did. I wish I could step up into that life and take my place next to Beckett. Haul his ass to the altar. Keep him in bed until I plant enough of my seed in him to finally think about something else for more than two minutes at a time.

My cock sure as hell likes the idea. But that monster needs to take a fucking time out.

He stirs a little in his sleep. He's got on plaid drawstring pajamas and a T-shirt. I can see the band of his boxers peeking above the waistband. Beckett snuggles deeper into me, and I feel the tree trunk in my pants grow even harder. This isn't right. I shouldn't want him so much. He's not trying to be sexy—he's just being himself. Just trusting me. I'm the biggest asshole.

"Why are you scowling?" His voice startles me as he sits up, stretching his neck. "Your foot hurting?"

"No, sorry. Just deep in thought."

He yawns and stretches, his shirt riding up a little more so I can see the soft hair on his stomach. I'm doomed. "Sorry I fell asleep."

"Nothing to be sorry for."

He cocks his head at me, his gaze inquisitive. "Are you mad at me? I'm sorry about leaning on you when I conked out. I hope you didn't think I was—"

"No."

"Really? Because your jaw is rigid, and there's a little tic thing happening in your mandible and you practically growled at me when you said no."

I take a deep breath. "I'm pissed at the asshole who made you feel bad. That's all."

He pulls his legs crisscrossed (he does yoga three times a week), getting comfortable, and I feel this weird feeling of pride that he's settling in to talk to me. Like we're friends. Like this could be what we did every night if we always lived together. Him sitting cross-legged on the couch looking at me like I had all the answers.

A guy could get used to it.

Don't.

"You should help me," he says.

"Help you what?"

"Figure out what I'm doing wrong. With men. Like a class...Real Man Seduction 101. You could teach me how to entice a guy like you."

Holy fuckballs.

"What are you talking about?"

"I mean like how *women* do for you. I know *I* couldn't entice a guy like you since I don't have boobs." He shakes his head. "I'm not doing something right. I need a guy's perspective. Someone who will be honest with me and steer me the right direction. I want to know how to get and keep the interest of a guy like you."

"A guy like me?"

He nods. "Yeah, a guy like you. What do the women do that get your attention?" He looks at me and pales. "You have total resting bitch face or you're pissed. Why is this making you mad?"

I try to relax my face, but he's mistaken about the anger. I'm not mad. I'm feeling about ninety-percent caveman right now. I don't want to scare him or make him uncomfortable, but I want to pull him under me and take him. Hard. It's bad enough he just asked me to help him, but help him get with another guy? Every cell in my body is rebelling like it's wrong. Like he belongs to me and me alone. And like I should show him with my cock who he belongs to.

I take a deep breath and will my muscles to loosen the fuck up. "What is a guy like me?"

"Are you fishing for compliments, roomie?" He tosses a pillow at me. "Well, aside from being a sexy alpha, you're confident. In charge. You know how to take care of things. You're a real man. You're honest, straightforward. You don't ask people out and then text them when you change your mind. You're like a superhero or something. When I'm with you, I feel secure, like nothing could hurt me. Like you'll take care of me. That's how I want to feel. That's how I want to make my future boyfriend feel when he's with me."

That's how he wants to feel with another guy.

But shit, he thinks I'm sexy.

"I think you deserve a guy better than me, Becks. I wasn't raised right. No role models. A series of strange men who would pretend to be my buddy for three weeks or as long as they could handle being with my mom and then they were gone. She was...unstable. And some of those guys...let's just say the sooner they left the better. She wasn't good at picking winners. It wasn't until your brother came along that I even had a real friend."

His face goes all soft. "I didn't know that. I guess we never talked about family before."

"Not much to say." I don't want his pity, that's for sure. But I do like all his attention focused on me like this. He has a way of making me feel like a better person than I am.

"My folks are great. A little...old-fashioned and always more broke than not. But Cam and I had good examples. I want a relationship like theirs." He sighs. "But I can't seem to find the right guy."

"You're setting your bar too low. That's your problem with men. It's not you; it's them. You're dating the wrong ones, is all."

He shakes his head. I want, God do I want, to show him how amazing I think he is. I don't have the kind of words he needs. The ones he deserves. Someone who has a better education than I do is who he should be looking at. Someone who has better manners and can be a real partner. A guy who'll give him all the babies he wants. Someone who knows how to love.

And whoever that asshole is, I hate him for being what Beckett needs. What he's really looking for. I hate him for not being me.

"I'm dating the guys who ask me out. If they are the wrong ones, then I need help finding the right ones to ask. And maybe I need to be more like you...more...I don't know...alpha."

I need off this couch. Out of this room.

"You just need to be yourself. That's all. You don't need to do a damned thing to be desirable. You already are."

He's turtling up because he doesn't believe me. I can see him withdrawing. His body curls into itself as he pulls his knees up and hugs them. "I get it. I shouldn't have asked for your help. It's weird."

"Becks, look at me."

He does and, fuck, I'm lost. Those sweet baby-blues are so sad. I can't walk away from him like this. Not when all he needs is for me to help him find his confidence.

"You're amazing the way you are. You're already a catch."

"You don't want to help me. I get it. It's okay."

"I didn't say I didn't want to help you."

"So, you will then?"

This is not good. I can already tell. He looks like Christmas morning.

"What exactly do you want me to do, Beckett?"

He gets this mischievous grin I haven't seen before. "A makeover. I mean, yeah, also you'll need to take me to a gym and show me..." He makes a hand wave over me. "...how to get all that going on. But first...we're going to the mall."

I groan.

"The mall?" I fucking hate the mall.

"You said anything. Besides, you're supposed to get a little exercise for that foot every day. We'll get some walking in, and then you can prop it up the rest of the day."

"What do you want at the mall?"

"An outfit or two that doesn't make me look like a kindergarten teacher would be nice."

"You *are* a kindergarten teacher." Why doesn't he want to look like one? I like the clothes he wears. The way he always looks ready for a hug.

"I want to entice a man into bed, Matthew. I need him to look at me like I'm a sex-toy made for pleasure, not a prissy teacher."

Fuck. Me.

CHAPTER FOUR

BECKETT

As we walk through the mall, I'm sort of pretending that Matthew is my boyfriend. Just imagining what it would be like to have him as mine. I know it's a fantasy, but I indulge anyway, noting how women, and one really hot dude, eye-fuck him as we go by. They aren't even hindered by the cane.

He doesn't seem to notice them. Which makes me wonder what it takes to get him to pay attention. What does he find attractive?

"Okay, so, what do you think I might be doing wrong?"

"Well, judging by the way you were talking to the that barista, who was not gay by the way, you're not doing anything *wrong*. You're just not putting it out there that you're worth any effort."

I stop and sip my cold brew. "How do you know he wasn't gay?"

"He just wasn't."

We resume. "So, how do I do what you're saying?"

"You need to exude more confidence. Own your intentions. If you want to ask a guy out, you need to show it from your approach. You need to be direct, confident."

"Show me."

His eyebrows might go past his hairline at this.

"Pretend I'm a girl."

He rolls his eyes. "Fine. Go sit over there. I'll come to you."

Down, boy. I have to remind myself he is doing this to help me, not give me spank bank material.

I sit on the bench, and he makes eye contact with me. Direct eye contact. I swallow. That is potent stuff, his eye contact. His eyes never leaving mine, he walks, in no particular hurry, over to me. His cane actually makes him a little hotter. Like a gentleman's cane. Though there's something in his eyes that is so not gentlemanly.

He gets to me and drops to his haunches and picks up a pen. "You didn't drop this, but I came all the way over here to give it to you."

My hand fumbles on my iced drink as I take the pen. "Thank you."

"You're a very attractive man. I'd like to take you to dinner."

My mouth opens and closes. I need to pull it together and make him work for it. *Pretend you are worth it*. "I don't even know you."

"Notice how I'm keeping the pitch of my voice low and controlled?" I nod. How could I not? His voice is one of the hottest things about him. "That shows people that I'm someone in control of myself in my surroundings. That I can handle myself. That's a turn on to someone who likes alphas. I'm steady, relaxed. Confident."

"Yeah, yeah you really are." I can't breathe.

"I'm going to keep eye contact with you, except for when I occasionally dip my gaze to your lips and back." He shows me. "What does that make you think of?"

"Kissing." Oh God, what would that be like?

"That's right, kissing. See, Beckett? I've done nothing self-conscious in front of you. No stammering, no raising my voice, no cheesy pickup lines. Just straightforward, confident conversation. And you're thinking about kissing me." The corner of his mouth quirks up when I nod.

I shake my head and smack him. I need to not get caught up in his pretend flirting. "Then what happens?"

"The person I'm talking to usually gives me little physical cues that they are receptive. Innocent touches." He brushes lint of my shirt. "They tilt their head a little, baring their throat to me. They lick their lips." The moment he says it, I lick mine. I can't even help it.

He stands up, and I try to blink away the fuzzy feelings. I see a woman in the shop across from the bench watching us.

"Underwear," I say, getting up and walking towards the store.

"What?" he asks.

"Let's go in here."

He looks at me like I'm sprouting another head. "Why do you want to go into the lingerie shop? You don't...I mean it's fine if you do..."

"No!" Oh my God. I wish a sinkhole would open up right now and take me out of my misery. "I'm gay but I'm not into wearing women's underwear."

He looks relieved. "Okay, then why are we talking about this?"

I nod to the pretty woman near the window adjusting bras on a rack. "She was totally eye-sexing you. I need you to show me how you flirt with a woman."

"But—"

I drag him into the store.

He's obviously very uncomfortable.

"Okay, when the salesgirl asks, we're here so I can buy my girlfriend a birthday present. While I'm looking, you make a move on her."

"This is a terrible idea."

I know. But I need a reminder that this isn't real life.

"Why? She's pretty. She was looking at you like you were her favorite candy. Just show me how you make the first moves. I need to see how it's done again."

He palms my shoulder and leans down so we're at face level. "Beckett—"

A too-beautiful-to-be-a-shopgirl woman greets us, and I immediately want to slink out. Her name tag says *Leslie,* and when she asks how she can help me, my tongue ties.

It seemed like such a good idea at the time.

She's eyeing Matthew like a snack but pauses at his hand still on my shoulder. She gives me a secret wink.

"My buddy wants to buy something that will knock his girlfriend's socks off," he tells her when I still haven't answered. "But all I know about lingerie is what I think will look good on my floor."

And now I ache with this strange jealousy that makes no sense. I imagine Leslie greeting Matthew in a corset when he comes home after a long, hard day. Matthew ripping lace off her body. His body covering her while scraps of expensive lingerie litter the floor around their bed.

I want to punch something. Or pull Leslie's hair, even though she seems kind of nice, actually.

I catch Matthew's gaze and worry that he can see my thoughts. But other than his normal, intense stare, all seems okay.

Leslie aka Supermodel Shopgirl smiles at him. "You two just made my day. This is my favorite part of the job. We have some things you'll love." She shoos Matthew over to the little couch set up for waiting and pulls me into a beautiful dressing room in the back, snagging a clipboard and tape measure on our way.

"Um...why are you measuring me?" I ask her.

She gets this puzzled look on her face. "I thought...you guys looked...I'm sorry. Are you really here shopping for a girlfriend? The way he was looking at you, I thought it was code for...you."

I blink. "No! We're both straight. And not into crossdressing."

She gives me the "Sure, Jan" look.

"We're not...we're not a thing. He's not my boyfriend, really."

Her perfectly arched eyebrows raise. "Maybe not yet, but my gosh, the way he looks at you made me feel butterflies."

She's nice. Doesn't look crazy. Doesn't seem stupid. And probably has way more experience with men than I have, but there's no way she's right about that. "How did he look at me?"

"Like he wanted to drag you into his cave. Seriously, I think he's got it bad for you."

I shake my head. "He thinks of me like a brother."

She purses her lips and shakes her head like I'm the one with a screw loose. "No, honey. No, he doesn't."

"Look, your gaydar is running about 50/50 today. Yes, I'm gay. Matthew is not. He's helping me by showing me how to be more like him. He's straight. He's here to get your phone number."

"And that's okay with you?"

I shrug. "Well, yeah. We're just roommates."

Leslie purses her lips and does this little hair flip thing that is wasted on me. "Okay. Then I'm going to bring a few things back and pretend I'm modeling them for you. If you're sure about me giving your man my number..."

"He's not mine."

He would be so embarrassed if he knew how often I pretended he was. How when I made him dinner, I'd fantasize about what it would be like to be married to him. How I think about what it would be like if he didn't go to the guest room at night but instead into the master suite with me like it was our room. Our bed.

But that's not real life either.

Real life is me being his wingman while he picks up Supermodel Shopgirl. God. What if this is the cute story I have to tell during their wedding toast? How I pretended to be shopping for lingerie for a non-existent girlfriend the day they hooked up.

I need to focus because there is no way in hell I'm going to their wedding as a single man.

I should have asked Supermodel Shopgirl to be my mentor instead.

CHAPTER FIVE

MATTHEW

We've been in this shop for a long ass time. I don't know what they're doing back there.

When the salesclerk, Leslie, joins me on the couch, I'm prepared for her to hit on me. It happens sometimes. I'm pretty good at letting the girls down easy, but Beckett might be watching so he can take notes on my technique.

This is one fucked up situation.

But instead, Leslie pats my knee in a very nonsexual way. "I think Beckett needs your advice."

"My advice? I don't know anything about lingerie. That's sort of your department."

"Maybe advice is the wrong word. I think he needs encouragement. He's feeling a little...well, confused. You should go talk to him. Set him straight. Or...better yet, tell him the truth about being gay."

My whole body tenses.

"Sweetheart, my gaydar is never wrong. Why haven't you told him the truth?"

I size her up, wondering how much to divulge. "It's complicated."

"You're not doing him any favors by pretending you are straight right now. Man up and tell him the truth."

My skin flushes hot at the thought of going back there and into a dressing room with him. Why is he even in one? "I'm not sure your other customers would appreciate two dudes in a dressing room."

"This is our dead time. He thinks I'm picking out lingerie to try on for him and giving you my phone number. You're both ridiculous. Go talk to him."

I pull the collar of my T-shirt away from my neck because it feels like it's choking me. The walk to the dressing room feels like the Green Mile, and I cough lightly and tap on the door. "Becks? Uh, Leslie sent me back here. You need anything?"

He opens the door and my heart stops.

"Where's Leslie? Did she already give you her number? I was supposed to watch."

I can't do this anymore. I push in and close the door behind me.

"Beckett, I'm gay."

I can't believe I'm coming out to my roommate in a women's lingerie dressing room.

He opens his mouth but no sound comes out. He closes it. Tries again. "Wait, what?"

"I'm gay. I don't like girls." I add, "That way."

"I...I...didn't know. I just assumed...wait, did Cameron know?"

"Yeah. Cam knew."

Beckett gets a look on his face that would break my heart if I had one. "He didn't know about me. I've wondered how he would have reacted. I didn't come out until after he died."

This I can help him with. "Cameron loved you. And all he wanted was for you to be happy. To have a good life. He wouldn't have cared."

I hope he believes that. Cam never gave two shits about my preference for dick.

"Why didn't you tell me? Are you in the closet?"

I shake my head. I was never in the closet. Not really. "I didn't want you to feel intimidated. It seemed easier to just go with it when you assumed I was straight. That way you would feel comfortable being cooped up in the condo with me over the summer. Since I'm alpha and you're omega." I take a deep breath. "This doesn't change things between us, I hope. I'm not going to cross any lines. You know that, right?"

"Because I'm not your type. Yeah, I understand."

He's staring at me, but his eyes look like they aren't really seeing me. I feel like he's upset. He doesn't actually wish…?

No, man. He doesn't. I'm just thinking with my cock. Trying to justify the way I want him.

"I'm not anyone's type."

"That's not true. We just…don't make sense. I'm not the kind of guy you're looking for. And we're roommates. That makes things complicated. Not to mention Cameron."

His jaw squares, and he turns his back to me. In the mirror, he's got his gaze locked with mine like a tractor beam from *Star Trek*. I'm not sure I have the kind of strength required to disengage.

"So I guess this changes our plan of attack then, yeah? We can stop playing this little game, and you can just go with me to a gay bar tonight and show me exactly what I need to do to get laid."

Does he have some sort of killer instinct? Talking about other men getting to be with him when I won't?

I take a step so that I'm directly behind him, but not touching him. Just a breath of space between us. His sugary scent teases me, but his eyes are locked with mine in the reflection. The tension weighs down on us like the air before a storm breaks.

From the corner of my eye, I can see his chest moving rapidly, like he's breathing fast and shallow. He gets this look. This knowing look and suddenly, I'm the one who's breathing too fast.

"So, if I wanted a guy just like you, but not you, to be interested in me, what do I need to change?"

The sassy little brat knows exactly what he's doing. He's not nearly so naïve as I thought. As soon as he learned I was gay, I think he knew, instinctively, that the reason I didn't tell him wasn't to protect him. It was to protect me.

He knows he's got the box of matches in his hand, now. But how badly does he really want to start this fire? Because I'm barely a spark away from inferno.

"You don't need to change; you're perfect," I tell him. He starts to disagree, but I splay my hand over his abdomen and yank him against me, letting him feel how hard he's made me. He gasps. "Don't argue with me. When a man like me compliments you, you say 'thank you.'"

His eyes go wide at the sudden change in my tone, but he whispers, "Thank you."

Oh man. The way he submits so fast ratchets up my desire.

And that's it. I'm fucking tired of fighting this. Fighting him. Fighting fate.

But I'll play his little game, if he wants.

"You really want to learn how to seduce a real man, Becks?" My fingers flex and curl over his stomach. "You want me to teach you, teacher?"

He nods shyly, our gazes still locked in the mirror.

"You need to tell me then. Tell me what you want. I want to hear the words on your lips."

"I want—" he starts but has to clear his throat. "I want you to teach me how to seduce a man like you, Matthew. I want to know how to get a guy like you into my bed. How to keep him there." He might be shy, but I don't know if my assessment that he's naïve was ever right. It seems like he knows what buttons to push on me. "I want you to help me lose my virginity."

His words are revving the engine inside me, getting me ready to take my foot off the brake and do what I've been dreaming of since I moved in with my sexy roommate. His body is tempting me, all his hard planes begging to be marked by my callused hands, my stubble, my cum. But it's his eyes that make me craziest right now. I could get lost forever in them. They're full of wonder and a little bit of fear.

I like that. Maybe I'm a dick for getting off on that. But I like that honeyed fear in his expression a little too much. I spent so many years protecting him, never knowing I'd be the biggest danger he faced.

He's trembling against me, sending little sparks up and down my body wherever we touch. He makes me burn so good, so hot.

I rest my chin on his shoulder, my other hand stroking down his arm leaving a trail of goose bumps wherever it sweeps across his skin. "If we do this, no more of this mall shit."

"Do what?" he asks.

"I'm going to teach you everything you need to break a man, baby."

He arches his neck a bit, and I can't tell if it's a subconscious move or if he knows he's driving me crazy. But I can't resist and lick his skin. His body tightens then goes slack, like I've turned his bones into Jell-O with the touch of my tongue.

I can't pull back the groan as it escapes my throat.

"I don't want to break a man, Matthew. I want to marry one."

I swear I start leaking pre-cum when he says that. Fuck. I should leave him alone. He wants a husband. A fucking groom. A baby daddy. And the very thought should have me running back to the safety of an oil rig. But instead, it sets off a primal drumbeat in my heart that echoes through my whole body.

Marry. Husband. Groom. Baby. The words should be a mood killer to a man with no intention of ever getting shackled, but instead, I see an image of him in a tuxedo, and I want to fuck him more than I want to breathe.

"Break him first. Then you can do whatever the hell you want to him, and he won't fucking care."

He's got this serious look on his face, like he doesn't think he has the power. Like he doesn't have me wanting to tear out of my own skin because it's so tight on me. Constricting.

I grasp his arms roughly and pull him into me hard, my erection poking him, showing him with my body what is difficult for me to say. His eyes take in the whole picture of us in the mirror. I can't hide my predatory gaze or the lead pipe in his back.

It's going too far. Getting too close. There's no way he won't see everything I want to hide.

We hear voices getting closer, and I remember where we are.

He leans back further into me. "I promise I'll do whatever you say if you teach me how to seduce you."

"A man like me, you mean."

"Of course. A man *like* you."

I spin him around, holding him by the shoulders as he jerks his chin up. My mouth is about to go crashing into his. I'm already anticipating the sweet flavors of his lips. I bend down, a trace of air between our mouths.

"Matthew? Beckett? My coworker's lunch is over, and the store is getting busy." Leslie's warning pierces the lusty thoughts I'm having, and I set Beckett a foot away from me.

Beckett stares at me for a second before answering Leslie. "Okay, thanks."

The beast inside roars his displeasure, but it's for the best. I need to help Beckett figure this shit out and move on because I am not the kind of man he needs. He wants a groom. A husband. A life filled with children.

All I can offer him is a lot of going nowhere at top speed.

CHAPTER SIX

BECKETT

After things got so heated in the dressing room, I wasn't sure what to expect. I think he would have kissed me if we had another thirty seconds of time before the interruption.

But Matthew returned to normal by the time we got home. No more growly, domineering hot alpha. To my utter and complete disappointment.

I don't want to act like nothing happened, but my pride is insisting that I don't show him how much he affected me. I can't deal with the rejection and still live here in this house with him. So, I'll just pretend the rejection isn't happening. That nothing out of the ordinary is happening. We're just roommates. Friends.

I still can't believe he is gay. My crush is gay, and I didn't even know it. No wonder I'm having a hard time dating. I have zero gay instincts. I wish there was a manual or something.

And it doesn't escape my notice that he chose not to tell me until he was literally cornered in a small dressing room with me. He can say it was for my benefit, so I wouldn't feel awkward or intimidated by him. But I think he just realized I had a crush, and if he gave me any straw to grasp at, I would. Obviously, he was right.

I'll figure out my guy problems without him. It's what I should have done to begin with. No more fantasizing about the hot guy I live with. No more pretending he's mine. No more remembering how hard he made me in the dressing room. How hard he was in there, too.

I'm changing strategies. Instead of having Matthew help me get to date number three with a man so I can sleep with him and lose my virginity, I'm going to just go out and get laid tonight. Maybe once I cross first-time sex off my bucket list, I'll be able to concentrate on meeting someone with relationship qualities because my lack of experience won't be hanging over my head. I was wrong in thinking that it should mean something and to wait for the right guy. I am holding myself back. Someday, I'll have sex with someone I love, I hope. I still want to find my future husband, if such a man exists. Find out what it feels like to have a child of my own growing inside me.

But tonight, I need to have sex with someone willing and able, and not worry about what Future Beckett wants. I have to stop hoping for what isn't going to happen with Matthew, too.

I slide out of my room quietly, hoping he's still napping on the couch where I made him rest his foot after walking around the mall.

"You're walking like Elmer Fudd when he was hunting wabbits." Matthew's voice startles me as I'm reaching for the doorknob. "Are you sneaking out for a reason?"

Yes, I'm sneaking out because I don't want to face him. So much for that plan.

I turn. "I wanted you to rest. I left a note for you on the fridge."

He stretches, his massive arms reaching into the air, and his heavily lidded eyes are so sleep-sexy that I wish I could curl up with him and join him in a nap. Or other bedtime activities. But no. Not going there. Not thinking about that. Not anymore. Not after he treated me like someone he could worship in front of that mirror and then turned it off the minute we left the store.

It's humiliating, really.

"Where are you going?" he asks.

"Out."

He raises his eyebrows. So I lift my chin in defiance. I don't have to tell him where I'm going. He's not my keeper.

"You have a date or something?"

I'm tempted to tell him yes, just to see if he gets jealous. But I won't. We are done playing games. "I'm going out with friends. I'll probably crash at Jenn's, so I'll see you tomorrow."

His demeanor changes. Tenses. His face goes stone cold. "What's going on?"

"Nothing."

"You're acting weird."

"I'm really not. Just going out. Wicket is playing at The Dive, and I've told you how much Jenn likes to watch her boyfriend's band play live."

He stands up, testing his foot. "You've told me Jenn likes to make sure nobody hits on her boyfriend at Wicket's shows."

I smile. "That too." We don't say anything for a beat too long, making it super awkward. I hate this, the way things feel weird between us. I wish I hadn't had a taste of what it feels like to be wanted by him. It makes the absence of it ache in my heart.

"You want me to give you a ride? I can pick you up so you don't need to worry about driving."

"No, that's okay. I'm meeting Jenn at her house, and she's driving tonight. I'll just crash there..." Or somewhere else, maybe, if all goes according to plan. It's harder to imagine going someplace with another man when Matthew is right here in front of me. But that's exactly why I have to do it. I can't keep pretending he's mine. He barely said two words to me before his nap. And now I dread whatever he might say because it obviously isn't what I want to hear. I need to let him go.

"About today..."

I hold my hand up. "It's okay. I understand."

"You do?"

I nod. "We got carried away. It was emotionally intense because my brother is dead and I never got to come out to him, but you did." I'm making it so easy for him to reject me without hurting my feelings. "No harm, no foul though, right?"

"Becks..."

"I have to go. I'll see you tomorrow. I took a casserole out of the freezer. You can just pop it in the oven."

"Becks..."

I pause, but he doesn't fill the silence. And that tells me what I need to know.

"Bye, Matthew."

I don't say, *the next time you see me, I won't be a virgin*. But I very much hope that it's true. For both our sakes.

CHAPTER SEVEN

MATTHEW

I don't even know what just happened but I know I don't like it. I hate it, as a matter of fact.

I screwed up today. I know what I want. I know what he wants. What I don't know is how to live with myself if we both get what we want. So instead, I acted like nothing happened in that dressing room, and now he thinks I don't want him. It might be easier if I didn't—but I sure as hell don't want him believing that he isn't desirable.

I'm doing pull-ups to kill time and work out some energy when my mind strays to what he's doing tonight. He was hiding something from me. As I conjure up the ways I think he might be reacting to being shut down from me after I worked him up, I don't like where my mind goes.

He isn't going out to keep his friend Jenn company tonight. He's going out to make bad decisions. I can feel it. I should have seen it in his eyes earlier.

Fuck. I never should have come on to him in the dressing room. But I did. I was like some asshole staking a claim to him, and then I let him dangle in the wind not knowing where he stood. I'm the worst kind of jerk. He deserves so much better than me.

And I think he's going to go looking for it tonight.

Maybe that would be best.

But what if he's too upset and not thinking clearly? What if he puts himself in a dangerous position to prove something to me? The Dive isn't a gay bar. If he comes on to the wrong guy, he might get the shit kicked out of him or worse.

I shake my head. He's been out long enough to know the dangers. He's with friends. He'll be fine.

Fucking Cameron. Why did he ask me to take care of Beckett? He knew exactly how unsuited for the job I am. He had to know he couldn't trust me with his baby brother. He would kick my ass if he saw how I treated him. He'd slit my throat if he could see my thoughts about him.

Fucking Cameron, why'd you have to die?

I shower. I eat. I try to watch a game. I find my keys. I drive to the bar. I curse myself the whole way.

He's the first thing I see when my eyes adjust to the dim interior at The Dive. There's very little light in the joint, but what there is attaches to him, singling him out to me. He's the most handsome man I've ever seen. In all the times I've looked at him, how did I not realize that?

I've never been in over my head with a guy before. But I'm drowning in him. I don't even want to be rescued.

He's talking to some punk. His hand is pretty close to Beckett's drink, and I'm worried that the guy thinks he's going to put something in it. Beckett is paying attention, though, and slides his hand over the top of the glass while he's pretend-laughing at something the punk says.

I know his real laugh, his real smile. And that ain't it.

I move through the crowd with him in my sights. My heartbeat is loud in my ears. He's my prey, and I'm a goddamned hunter. I don't think I can stop this now. That beast is back, and he won't be satisfied until Beckett is ours.

I've heard this is how it is for alphas when they find the right omega for them, but I always thought it was some kind of urban legend. I've never had these kinds of primal, instinctive feelings before. I've never felt like there was part of me that was more animal than human.

I feel that beast now, though.

As I get closer, I notice how tight Beckett's pants are, and I know I'm not the only one appreciating it. I was right. He is looking for trouble tonight. I guess he's going to find it.

I'm going to give him a hell of a lot of trouble.

He senses me staring at him and looks up, his lips drawing into a shocked "O." He grabs his friend's arm to get her attention, and Jenn gets that same surprised look. The dude talking to him takes one look at me and moves away.

Good choice, motherfucker.

"Matthew?" he says when I reach him.

"I'm taking you home." The words are raw, and I didn't mean to say them. That damn beast inside got control for a second.

He narrows those eyes that shoot dagger-glares at me. "I don't think so. I'm happy here. And you don't get to tell me what to do."

"That's not what you were thinking earlier today."

He sputters, and I don't blame him. What the hell is my problem?

Jenn grabs his arm. "Do you want me to call somebody?" she asks Beckett, eyeing me nervously.

I'm glad he has a friend who worries about him. "You don't ever need to protect him from me."

She and Beckett exchange an entire conversation using just their eyes, and then Jenn tells us she's going to go find her boyfriend. Beckett might be pissed, but he's not scared.

After she leaves, Beckett gives me a look that might work on his students, but doesn't do shit except get me hotter for him. I am on fucking fire. Then he downs his drink the way he probably learned in college.

He sets his empty glass on the bar behind him. "You should go. I want to stay here."

"Thought maybe we could have another lesson tonight." My words are meant to be light, but I know they don't sound like it. I'm thirty seconds away from throwing him over my shoulder and hauling his ass out of here.

He shakes his head like he's dismissing me. "I changed the course objectives."

"Oh yeah? What are they now?"

"I decided I don't need to get to date number three. A one-night stand to take the edge off is a better plan."

The air in my lungs freezes. I don't think he's bluffing. "You're just going to pick some random guy and get it over with then, huh?"

Beckett shrugs. "It's not your problem. I'm sorry I dragged you into it."

"So, who's the lucky guy?" I look around. "Tell me is isn't the punk I scared off already."

I've never seen the mask he's wearing now. Tough guy. Tired of my shit. "I think I'll have better luck if you leave."

Like. Hell.

"Why don't you give me a dry run? Work out the kinks. Pretend I'm the guy. Show me how you're getting me in your bed."

He narrows his eyes. "You're being a real asshole, you know that?"

Yeah, baby. I know that.

"Just show me, Beckett. You wanted my advice, remember? You wanted me to help you figure out what you were doing wrong."

He glances around, probably looking for a drink to throw in my face, but everyone around us is holding theirs and his glass is empty. With a sigh, he reaches out to me and straightens the collar of the flannel I'd thrown on. Then he gives me a little smile and leans in to smell my neck. "I like that cologne. What's it called?" he asks.

I'm not wearing cologne.

"I...ah..." I don't know why I'm tongue-tied.

"I'm wearing a new one, too. Do you like it?" He offers me his neck, so I lean down to sniff him, and it seems like the same cologne he's been wearing that usually drives me nuts. It's a light scent, not particularly evocative. But it's sort of...elusive. I can only ever get hints of it at home, and it makes my gut clench for a deeper pull of the scent.

As he brings his hand down, he skims the front of my shirt. "Well, do you like it?"

"I...yeah...sure."

He slides his hand around my wrist and reads the time on my watch. "It's getting late." He licks his lip and stares at mine. "Luckily, tomorrow is Sunday and I don't have to do anything but lounge around in bed all day."

Now I'm picturing him sliding around in my sheets. And that's his plan. He's...he's *flirting* with me.

Well played, Becks. He took fucking notes from our lesson in the mall. The innocent touches, the offering me his neck. And now I'm ready to bend him over a bar stool. From innocent flirting. What has he done to me?

I am not the in-control guy full of confidence and swagger that I was this morning in that mall.

He lets go of my wrist and leans against the bar on his elbows, which thrusts his chest out. I step between his legs, lean down into his space without touching him. I stare at his Adam's apple and grunt, which makes him swallow harder.

"You pick out this lucky man yet?"

He looks around the room like he's bored and shrugs. "Maybe the guy in the red shirt down there." He's tilting his head to the end of the bar, but I don't bother looking.

"You don't want him."

"No?"

I shake my head. "No." My heart is beating a primal beat, and my blood is too hot. "You want me."

He licks that lip again. "A guy *like* you, remember?"

His words, the echo of our conversation earlier, are like a bullet tearing its way through me. Reminding me how I treated him today. How no matter how hard I try, no matter what I do or don't do, I am going to hurt him.

My eyes move from that damn lip down to the column of his throat, where his pulse jumps like I'm touching him. I'm hard. Maybe harder than I've ever been.

"We're going home. Now." Before I can't stop myself from taking him here, in this bar, in front of God and everyone. Because I want to mark him. Claim him. And I want everyone to know he's mine. "You're going to break me tonight, Beckett. And I'm going to teach you how."

CHAPTER EIGHT

BECKETT

We don't speak much the whole way home. I don't want him to change his mind like he obviously did when we left the mall earlier today. But I also don't understand what happened to get him to come find me tonight.

He wants to teach me to break him. I'm not even sure I know what that means.

But I really, really want to find out.

We get into the house and are beset with uncomfortable silence. The kind that makes the ticking of the clock on the mantel sound like it's super loud. Before yesterday, we didn't ever have uncomfortable or awkward silences. It's sad. But if I went back in time, if I never told him I was a virgin or asked him for advice, then I never would have seen that hungry look in his eyes today. I never would have watched him prowl through a crowded bar looking for me so he could bring me home.

Does he even know how that affected me? If he'd have said, "Come with me," it wouldn't have been such a big deal. But no..."We're going home," means more. At least it does to me. Home means something, doesn't it?

But I can see he's rethinking this already.

If he thinks he can just keep yanking me around, he's got another thing coming.

"What was it that made you come find me tonight?" I ask. "Was it that you wanted me, or you just don't want anyone else to have me?"

His jaw squares, and he presses his lips into a firm line. "I'm supposed to be teaching you how to seduce a man, aren't I? I can't do that if you're not here."

A red haze clouds my vision. "Oh, right. I see. So, are you going to teach me how to fuck and then send me back to The Dive? Is that how this works?" He winces. "You could have just left me there tonight. I'd have figured it out on my own. I'm a smart man. College educated and all."

"I knew you were planning something rash. So I went there to stop you."

"Something rash?"

Whose voice was that? It couldn't have been mine. It sounded like a deep, gravelly rumble. Not my kindergarten teacher voice for sure.

"Something rash," he repeats dully. But his body language is clear that he already regrets what might happen next. He doesn't want me—he wants to take care of me, maybe. He doesn't want me to sleep with someone else, certainly. But that's not the same. And it's not enough for me.

"I don't believe this." I toss my phone and wallet on the table by the door. "Fine. You did it. You stopped me. Thank you for saving me from myself. You've done your good deed. It's too bad you have to keep acting like you want to have sex with me to get me to do what you want—but you're a real trooper for sticking it out. Don't forget to take your pill. I'm going to bed."

Tomorrow, I will look for an apartment. This isn't going to work for me anymore. I can't keep letting my desire for Matthew stop me from living my life, and I know I'll never give any other guy a real chance if I think there's even the smallest chance with Matthew.

And there isn't. He won't let there be. I don't know why he's so conflicted. I'm sure he'd never tell me. I try hard to tell myself it's his problem and not an extension of my normal man issues. But it's hard. It's so damn hard not to take it personally that something about me seems to repel men even if they seem all-in for a few minutes.

My throat is tightening, and I consider going for a run. I don't...run...very often. It's not my go-to stress reliever. But I need something to burn off this resentment taking over.

I make it halfway across the room when the steely band of Matthew's arm reaches around me and pulls me into his chest. "I'm sorry, Becks. I'm sorry I keep screwing this up."

God. He is so big and strong behind my back. I melt into him even though I don't want to. I can't stop craving his touch. "I don't understand what you want, Matthew. I don't think even you know."

"I know exactly what I want. I just don't feel like I should have it."

"Why?" I reach for his other hand, the one that isn't gripping me so hard into him, and bring it to my cheek. I press my face into it like a cat. "Why shouldn't you have what you want?"

I kiss his palm, and he gasps. The world spins as he turns me in his arms and walks me backward to the wall so quickly I don't think my feet touch the ground. I'm trapped between him and the wall.

The expression on his face is one of near agony, though. "I don't deserve you, Beckett. You're so good and nice. I'm not the guy for you. The things I want to do to you..." He slams his eyes closed as a shiver wracks his body. "I want to defile you. Do you understand? Rough and raw and filthy, baby. That's how I want to take you."

His eyes open again, and the way he is looking at me is positively barbaric. All that masculine power directed at me is overwhelming. My pulse kicks up as a new need claws at me from the inside. I want him to take me. Possess me. I want all that potent male energy covering my body, filling me up.

He groans, and I blink out of my little trance just as his mouth kicks into a feral grin and he says, "You like that, don't you?" He pushes me against the wall harder so I can feel his solid erection. It's really hard and really big. Really, really big. "Fuck. You're hard right now, aren't you?" My face heats because he's right. "I'm going to take you tonight. I'm going to feel your hot ass clenching around my cock. I'm going to make you lose your fucking mind. Make you crave my dick like a drug. Maybe then you'll understand how much I fucking want you."

I moan, the sound so full of longing I should be embarrassed, but I'm not. "Yes. Yes, please, Matthew. I need you so much."

He buries his face in my neck and groans again. "You smell so good. I can't get enough of you. I bet you taste good, too. I bet I'm going to get addicted to the taste of your cock."

I arch into him then, angling the best I can so his cock will rub against where I need him most. There are too many clothes between us, though, and I exhale a frustrated sound when the friction isn't enough.

"You getting greedy, baby? You want my cock in you already?"

"Yes. Please."

He pulls back and looks into my eyes. "I haven't even kissed you yet." Despite the primal fire burning in his eyes, he seems to bank it when he runs his finger from my temple down my jaw so gently I am surprised I can feel it. "You're so perfect."

He presses his lips to my temple, then follows the path his finger made with soft kisses. If he didn't have me pinned to the wall, I don't think my legs would hold me. The sweet kisses undo me in a way even his dirty talk didn't. They are reverent, adoring. That this is the same man who wants to defile me makes me the luckiest guy in the world right now. Because I want it all. I want his sweetness and I want his filthy, filthy passion. I want him to tear me apart and kiss me back together.

When he gets to my lips, he cups my jaw in those big, rough hands and takes small sips of my mouth like I'm a fine wine to be savored. I'm trying to be patient because these kisses are wonderful, but he's the spark to my tinder, and I know I'm about to burst into flames. I dart my tongue out for a taste of my own, and we combust around his untamed growl. He grinds his stiff cock into my groin and plunges his tongue into my mouth. And I take it. Oh God, do I take it. My fingers are clawing his biceps, but I'm unable to get him close enough while his mouth is basically fucking mine.

Thinking I'm smart, I lower my hands to his ass, pulling him harder into me so I can grind on that hard erection that has my name on it. On a guttural groan that sounds like it was pulled out of him, he stops kissing me long enough to grab my hands, pinning them to the wall on either side of my head. "You are going to make me come in my jeans if you keep doing that."

"So take them off."

"I have plans for you, baby. So you're just going to have to wait."

I struggle briefly to get control of my hands back but realize that just isn't going to happen. He's too strong. And he wants control right now. Which is delicious, if you ask me, so I stop struggling and cede to him. That fire flares in his eyes again when he feels me submit.

"Do whatever you want to me, Matthew. I'm yours."

There's a moment of complete stillness between us—like the one before a jaguar leaps on its prey. Calmly, almost too carefully, he brings my wrists higher above my head and transfers them both to one hand. He cups the back of my neck in the other and brings himself to eye level with me. It's intense, unlike anything I've ever felt, when he looks so deeply into my eyes I feel like he's seeing straight into my soul.

My pulse is racing, and something wild inside me is unfurling, beating at my bones and skin to be let out. I've never felt this way before. I don't even know how to express it.

Matthew swallows hard. "You're mine. You've been mine for a long time. I'm not going to fight it anymore, if this is what you want."

"Yes, yes, I want this."

"You need to be sure. Once I take you, Beckett, I'm never giving you up. You'll belong to me completely. Forever."

"And you'll belong to me, Matthew."

"Fuck, yeah, I will. God, that sounds so amazing." He leans his forehead on mine. "I feel like I've been fighting this so long, and I don't even remember why half the time."

If this is a dream, I don't want to wake up.

He's moved those lips to my neck. I had no idea it was such an erogenous zone on me, but I can't stop rocking my hips. He's breathing hard, like he's fighting to contain himself. But I want him wild. "Matthew—I know why I waited." I clutch his hair, bringing his gaze back to my face. "I'm still a virgin because I was waiting for you. All this time, it was you."

I see the change. If he were some kind of supernatural creature, his fur would come out or his fangs would pop. Instead, he growls and yanks the front of my shirt down hard, tearing fabric and sending buttons skittering across the carpet. He sucks my Adam's apple, and my body arches, my back bowing.

"You're mine," he tells me as he starts suckling my skin, sending sparks shooting through my whole body. "Tell me. Say it."

I can hardly catch my breath, but I say, "I'm yours. Yes. All yours."

Whatever rejection I was feeling before wasn't about him not desiring me. Knowing Matthew, he probably thinks he's not good enough for me. Or he's got some sense of honor that says he can't mess with his friend's little brother. But knowing that he's this hot for me, for my body, frees me in a way I've never felt.

I finally understand the power I have. He told me I could break a man like him. He probably didn't know I could put him back together, too.

I try to move my hands so I can touch him, but he's still got a strong hold on me. "Do you like this, baby?" He moves down my chest with wet kisses, stopping on my nipple. It's like a wire shocks me, jolting me. "Yeah, you like that. Does it make you hard?"

"Everything about you makes me hard, Matthew. Go ahead and check."

He gives me that feral grin again and bites my nipple. The shock of pain followed by the soothing lick of his tongue makes me cry out.

"Yes, oh God, yes!"

"You're my dirty little teacher, aren't you? All sweet words and cookies by day, and fucking filthy man by night. I'm going to learn all your secrets, baby. I'm going to master everything that makes you writhe and moan out in pleasure. I don't think you're ever going to get a full night's sleep again."

My legs are weakening with every syllable he utters. He undoes my jeans and snakes his hand down my pants. He grasps my cock and we both moan.

"Fuck, so much pre-cum. Such a good boy, getting ready for me." When he pulls his hand out and licks me off his fingers, I almost pass out I'm so turned on. "Jesus, you taste good. So good. I'll never get enough of you."

"Take me to bed, Matthew," I plead while I try to kick off my shoes.

"We haven't been on three dates yet, Becks. Don't you want to wait?" he teases even as we both groan at the contact and friction between our jeans while I try to maneuver my socks off.

"I don't want to wait." I reach up and suck on the skin under his jaw. "I want you to make me a man. I want to give you everything. Nobody's ever touched my ass before, Matthew." The guttural sound he emits gives me confidence that I've got him where I want him now. "You'll be the first."

"I'll be your fucking last." He yanks my pants down, taking my boxers with them. As I step out of the legs, he drops to his knees and plants his face between my legs, inhaling deeply, his nose pressed into my balls. I'm not used to this kind of raw intimacy, and I freeze up a little. He presses his cheek to my thigh and looks up at me. "It's all right, Becks. Just relax. I'm going to swallow your sweet dick until my mouth is your whole world and you forget your own name. Give me five minutes, and you'll never be shy with me again."

Well, I don't know about that, but I'm certainly willing to give him a shot. I stroke his hair while he's looking up at me. It's soft like silk, so strange on a man who's hard all over. He grabs my hand and kisses it.

He's like a god on his knees in front of me. Me! And he's smelling my dick like we're animals and kissing my fingers like I'm to be revered. I don't know how to deal with all these different sides of him, but when he rises up and takes my hand, it doesn't matter. He leads me into my room, and then I'm in the middle of my bed, and he's taking my shirt all the way off. And then comes his shirt.

I was laying back on the pillows, but I rise up to get me some of that. I want to touch all of him. He's so gorgeously made. Part giant maybe. Muscles honed by honest, hard work. Powerful, strong. I can't wait to feel the weight of him on top of me. I want to be surrounded by all that strength.

"Pants, Matthew. Take off your pants."

He stands up, his hand on the top button near the bulge straining the zipper. And then he shakes his head. "No."

CHAPTER NINE

MATTHEW

Beckett is on his knees in the middle of the bed, and I want to fuck him so hard that the bed breaks beneath us. But I'm not going to.

Not yet.

I can't take my pants off. I've gotten this far without really thinking of the logistics. In all my fantasies, it was never a problem. But I never thought we'd really get this far.

If I take off my pants, I'm going to scare the shit out of him.

I'm a big man. All the fuck over. One man uttered, "Urban legend," when he first saw me. I don't brag because I was born like this and didn't do anything to earn it. And having a monster cock isn't always an advantage. I got teased some in the locker room, but that part was never a big deal. Some guys, okay most guys, seem to be excited about it...at first. But it's sometimes a lot of work and sometimes, well, men give up.

And occasionally, I've been told it hurts too much to try.

I know it fits. I mean... it looks like it won't at first, but it *will* fit. If the dude is relaxed and lubricated enough. The guy staring at me is certainly willing. But he's an anal virgin. I've stayed far away from virgins in the past. For obvious reasons.

I don't want to hurt him. I'd kill for him. I'd die for him. I don't want to be the one who hurts him.

But I want him. I need to make him mine. But the idea of causing him pain almost makes me wish I could go soft and we could just cuddle all night.

But that isn't going to happen. The beast in my pants is ready to own him. The best I can do is go slow and keep him on edge enough to be distracted.

"Lay down, baby. Show me that sweet ass." My voice comes out thick.

My sweet schoolteacher looks disappointed that my jeans are still on, but he'll get over it. He reclines all the way and opens his legs.

"Your cock is the most mouth-watering thing I've ever seen." I get on the bed, my jeans too tight to move easily, and spread his legs further so I can get between them. I lift one, straightening it, and bring my mouth to the inside of his ankle, pressing soft, moist kisses there while I stroke up and down his hairy leg. "Your body was made for me. You turn me on so much."

I move up his leg slowly. When I finish exploring one leg, I start on the other. He's got a spot behind his knee that makes his whole-body shiver, so I explore there, experimenting with patterns and pressure until he brings his hands up to that gorgeous cock like he can't stop himself from playing. That's so sexy. I have to unbutton my jeans, or they will cut off circulation.

I move around his body, skipping where I want to be the most to massage his arms.

I kiss his stomach, bite it, suck it, tongue his belly button. "I fucking love your stomach. I think it's sexy as hell."

"My stomach?"

"Fuck yeah. But so are your elbows."

"My elbows?"

"Beckett, your body makes me hot because it's you. The way you laugh makes me hot. The way you sing when you don't know you're doing it makes me hot. The way you cook food and play Candy Crush and water plants makes me hot. I want to touch you all the time." I move up his body and kiss him. "Wait until you hear the things I want you to do with that mouth."

He raises up on his elbows. "Why are you still wearing pants, again?"

Because my gigantic dick is going to scare the fuck out of you.

"If my cock comes out, it'll be over too soon. I want to eat you." I push his shoulder gently so he lays back down. "Beckett?"

"Yeah."

"Lay down and show me your hole."

His eyes go round from shock, but his pupils dilate, letting me know that rough talk turns him on.

I lick his taint. "You're so sweet." I want in that ass. His eyes get big, wondering what dirty thing I'm going to do to him next as I move up to his balls and start sucking the sweet skin there. I'm making noises I can't control anymore as I continue to play with him. He's bouncing around, unable to keep his hips still. I stuff as much of his sac in my mouth as I can, like a glutton, pulling it deep into my mouth and moaning around it. He's so fucking perfect. I love the way he tastes, the sounds he makes. I let go of his balls and use my tongue on his ass, rimming the sensitive nerves there.

"Oh God. Oh God. You're going to make me come."

After I grab the lube from his nightstand, I press and dip my fingers into his hole, holding them there as he stretches around them.

"Such a dirty teacher." I'm working my fingers in and out of him and use my mouth to go at his dick. It slides in my mouth like a dream, and I swallow his knob and press his prostate until he roars and comes in my mouth. It's the most erotic feeling, all slick and warm on my tongue. I love the way he smells and tastes. I don't waste a single drop. I have always loved cum, but it's never tasted sweeter.

I keep him in my mouth until he's soft and relaxed. He's shivering a little, so I lay on top of him and roll us over so he's resting his head on my chest while he comes down from his high.

My cock is fucking aching. I'm probably going to blow a load in my pants because I can't keep this up. I still want to eat that ass more, though.

When he's breathing right again, I slide back down to paradise and give him a few slow licks. I leave his cock alone for a few more minutes, knowing he's sensitive, but I get my tongue everywhere else. I spread his legs as wide as I can and bury my tongue in his virgin hole. He's tight, and I'm worried again about hurting him. It's never far from my mind. He starts making those pretty sounds again, so I use my tongue like it's my dick and fuck him, getting as deep as I can.

Mine. He's all mine.

I can't stop thinking about how I'm going to be the first one in there. The last one, too. There's no way another man is ever getting near him. Not now. I can't get enough. I want to devour him, and I bury my face in him. He starts grinding on my face, and so I grab his ass and hold him to me as hard as I can, probably leaving marks on his butt as he starts bearing down and calling out my name.

He's wrung out now. As relaxed as he'll ever be, so that's when I ease off him and finish taking off my pants. When I get back on the bed, he opens his eyes lazily, and then sits up like he's seen an intruder.

"Oh my God," he says. His eyes get bigger and his face loses color. "You're..."

I look down at my Johnson. "Big. Yeah."

He blinks rapidly. "That is not big. That is gigantic."

Fuck.

"You're gonna have to make friends, Becks, or this isn't going to work."

"Okay, okay. Just give me a second to process this." He tears his eyes away from it to my face. "How...big...is?"

"Big enough." I don't know how to tell him that it's actually gotten a little softer since he started freaking out. I want to fuck him so bad, but I can't deal with hurting him. I don't see how I cannot do one or the other. "Do you trust me?"

"Of course I do."

"Do you still want to do this?"

His eyes meet mine, and then he launches himself across the bed and into my arms. "Matthew, you're all I want. Yes, I want you to fuck me. I promise."

My arms wrap around him. "You're not scared." He feels so good pressed against me, skin on skin.

"Of course, I'm scared. But I know you'll make it good for me. I trust you. And I believe in you."

CHAPTER TEN

BECKETT

That was the right thing to say.

Matthew's arms tighten around me, and he takes my mouth in a possessive, feral kiss. I melt into him, knowing where I belong even if it all feels so strange and uncertain to me. I've spent years feeling like there was something wrong with me, and then the hottest guy I could dream up has spent the last hour focusing on my pleasure. Telling me he wants me.

And now, I find out he's got the blue ribbon of all cocks. His is not a starter penis. And right now, it's pushing against my stomach as he kisses me. And the tingles start in my balls again, even though the thought of having him inside me is more than a little scary.

The kiss is getting more possessive. More dark and raw, and I feel an answering need inside when he delves his hand into my hair and tugs hard. The sharp sting with the deep kiss turns my blood to fire. I'm going to fly out of my skin and shoot like a star into the universe. Matthew's mouth moves lower, sliding up and down my throat. I want him to bite me, mark me.

"You're so fucking mine," he murmurs, nipping at my neck.

I'm coming alive again. This man and his dirty words and his need for me that he doesn't hide overwhelm my senses. His hands go lower and he squeezes my ass cheeks roughly.

"Such a juicy ass, baby. Made for my hands. I can't fucking get enough of you."

And then I am laying down, and he is on top of me. We are skin-to-skin touching from head to toe, and that big cock is sliding between our stomachs, rubbing against mine in a frot to end all frots. "You feel so good, Matthew. I love the weight of you on top of me."

He pauses and looks deeply into my eyes. Everything becomes so clear to me. He's been saying I'm his in that possessive way, but it isn't until this moment that I understand what that means. I mean, it's been hot to hear, and it turns me on when he's all dominating and alpha male with me, but it's now, naked in this bed, looking into his eyes, that I finally *get* it.

Yes, I'm his.

I belong to him. I belong *with* him.

And he belongs to *me*.

"Matthew."

"Yeah, baby?"

"I can't wait to feel you inside me. I want you to show me everything. Show me how it feels to belong to you."

He rests his head on my chest. "Fuck. I need you so much, but I don't want to hurt you."

I move my hips, sliding that cock between us. "I trust you. You'll make it good. You'll take care of me."

He shudders like the feeling is too much and returns his gaze to mine.

"Matthew, I love you."

He makes a low sound in his throat, and all his muscles tighten and bulge. He is so masculine, so virile. He's everything. My world narrows until it's just him.

"I can't resist you."

He pulls back and grasps that huge cock. It's intimidating for sure, but when he starts sliding against mine, dipping it between the cheeks of my ass, and tapping it against my hole, I moan with pleasure.

"I'm going to make you come so hard with this beast, baby. You'll be my cock slave, willing to do anything I say to get this back in you."

It's so heavy and perfect. "Yes, anything you want."

Show me how to break you, Matthew.

It is time to make friends with that beast, so I reach for it. I can barely get my hand around the whole thing, but I stroke it slowly and watch his eyes go heavy-lidded with pleasure.

His cock is wet from pre-cum and smooth like velvet. I want to rub it all over my body. I move it against my own now hardening again cock, and we both hiss in ecstasy. "I can feel you getting even harder. How is that even possible?"

"It's all you, Beckett. You're so sexy. Pure and filthy at the same time. You make me feel like an animal. You make me want to do things..." He breaks off when I squeeze us both together. He's dripping pre-cum now, lubricating the glide of my hands.

But I still don't feel like I know what happens next. Well, I do...but I don't. This is so much further than I've ever gone. I don't want to make some stupid blunder and ruin it. "What things do you want to do to me? Tell me."

"You want me to shock you, Becks? Tell you all the dirty things I'm going to do to you?"

Oh my God. I nod and rub the mushroom head against mine where I'm most sensitive. "Yes, tell me. Please."

"There isn't a part of you that won't belong to me. Be marked by me. I'm going to come inside you, fill you up with all my cum. My balls are heavy with it. Making so much of it to put in you."

He covers my hands with his, and we stroke us together. Then he gets the lube again and pushes my knees up and he notches himself at my opening. I try not to tense up. I know it will fit.

"I have condoms...but..." I lift my head and look at the baseball bat between his legs. "There is no way they would fit you."

He smiles, pleased, I think, that he has this problem. "I have condoms in my room." He looks down where his cock rests against my hole. "I get tested every six months. I haven't been with anyone for longer than that. A lot longer."

I try not to act too surprised. But wow. I really am. He's the kind of guy who is in hot demand. Plus, his libido seems pretty high. I can't imagine him going without that long. But then, I haven't seen him going out of his way to go out and get laid since we've been living together. I guess I just assumed.

I nod.

"You sure, Beckett?"

"Yes, you wouldn't lie to me."

"I would never lie to you. I'll always protect you. Always." He pushes into me a little more, just past the tight ring of my sphincter.

Now that I'm more accustomed to him, he's starting to feel really good inside me. I know it's just the tip, but I like it. He pushes in just a little more, stretching me. I don't ask him to stop. Another inch goes in. My heartrate jacks up.

His temples are sweaty, and his arms are tense from holding back. He's not pulling out. He's not going all in. We're in this weird limbo. My inner muscles clench around him, and we both make low noises in our throats. It feels so good. Too good.

"More," I groan. "Put it all in me."

He actually starts shaking. "You keep talking like that and I'm going to turn into a rutting animal. I'm just a man, Beckett. I can only resist temptation so long before I take what you are offering."

I dig my heels into his back.

"Fuck." His big hand covers more than half my face as he holds me still to take his kiss. Like I'd try to get away. His hold is possessive, and his tongue pushes into my mouth obscenely. He's fucking my mouth when he breaches me completely, pushing right through in one solid thrust, absorbing my shocked gasp in his mouth. I freeze up and then my instincts make me try to push him away, but he holds me still. I'm pinned to the bed by his dick, his hand holding my face to his, forcing me to take his kisses while my body adjusts to the intrusion.

"Breathe, baby."

"It hurts."

"I know, Becks. Just give it a minute, okay. Trust me?"

"Always."

"Oh baby, you don't know what that does to me. I love that you just keep giving me that sweet trust. I'll make it good. Don't worry. Just try to breathe and relax for a minute."

I've played around with a dildo before, I know he's right.

He kisses me again, and I concentrate on the way he tastes. The way his tongue feels against mine. My chest loosens up, and I can breathe again. I still feel incredibly full. Almost too full, but the sting is starting to ease, and when he shifts, we both gasp at the intense feeling.

"You're so tight. Feels so good. Are you doing okay?" He thrusts a little more.

My fingers gouge his shoulder. "Oh, yes. Start moving."

"You sure?"

I nod. "More," I assure him.

"Beckett, open your eyes and look at me."

I hadn't realized they were closed. I blink up at him. He looks concerned, but underneath there's this level of...ferocious is the only word I can think of. "I'm not all the way in. Do you understand? There's more."

"Oh. *Oh*." Good God. How big is this man? He still looks fierce, his face a mask of an angry warrior. "Are you mad at me?"

He relaxes his expression with what looks like great concentration. "No. Your ass is just tighter than anything I've ever felt. You're squeezing me so good. It's taking every ounce of control I have not to force you to take all of it. I want my cock in you to the hilt." He's gritting his teeth, forcing himself to go slow. "I want to impale you on it."

"Do it." He closes his eyes, still fighting his hunger. "Do you want me to beg?" He grunts. Well, I'm not above begging, not if it gets us what we both want.

I wrap my legs around him for more leverage, but I can't force him in the way he's holding himself. He's too strong. But I have a hunger, too. I want that cock. Bad. He may have fallen for a shy schoolteacher, but the man he just made wants all of him. He won't be denied.

"Matthew, I want you to make me yours. I need it, baby. Make me yours. Give me all that cock. Please. I'm begging you."

"Jesus Christ, you're killing me." He was no longer staying still, but his shallow thrusts weren't enough. Not for him. Not for me.

"Matthew, I love knowing we're doing this raw." He groans. "I love knowing when you come, you're going to fill me up. I can't wait to feel you gush inside—"

He shuts me up with a deep kiss, but it's almost playful. Heaven knows we're enjoying ourselves.

"That's not fair," I tell him when he lets me up for air.

"You're not playing fair. Talking dirty. Trying to make me come. You know I have to pull out, right? As much as I'd love to fill you up, I can't get you pregnant tonight."

I nod. "But it makes you hotter, doesn't it? Thinking about coming inside me?" Lord knows I'm suddenly having breeding fantasies.

"God, yes." He grits his teeth. "Stop talking about it."

"I don't know why you're fighting this so much."

He rests his forehead against mine. "I don't want it to be over."

"Matthew, it doesn't ever have to be over."

A pained look flashes across his face, and then he looks oddly peaceful. Like my words just sank in, and he has a new understanding. "I love you, Beckett," he says. "I'm done fighting it. You said you loved me, and I hope you meant it because you're mine now. I'm going to take care of you and keep you so satisfied, you'll never even think about what you might be missing out on." He thrusts all the way in, hard.

The action shocks me as I make sense of his words. And then nothing makes sense and all I can do is feel.

CHAPTER ELEVEN

MATTHEW

I'm a fucking animal, and it's all his fault. He did this, and I hope he's happy because I am not going to stop until there's so much of me leaking out of him that it will still be coming out tomorrow.

His heels dig into my ass and I let go, pistoning inside my man, while my hands grab whatever flesh I can. Jesus, I'm possessed. Nothing has ever felt so good. So right.

He's taking my cock like a champ. I know it's too much. Too big. I should slow down and go easy on that poor ass of his. But it feels so good, like it's trying to squeeze the cum out of me, his inner muscles clenching me tight.

I'm leaking so much pre-cum I can actually feel it coming out, mixing with the lube, coating the walls of his virgin ass. Goddamn. He's not a virgin anymore, though. He's mine.

I want to give him my baby. Right fucking now. My God. I've never needed anything more.

"You want my cum, baby?" I hold still, feeling like my entire life is hanging in the balance waiting for his answer. I grab his cock and jerk it wildly and he shouts as he starts to come again.

That's when I can't control the beast any longer. I shove it into him like a battering ram on a castle door. The headboard is banging into the wall. He's still coming, wetting my stomach and his, still calling out my name, lost in his pleasure.

"Take. All. Of. It." I slam into him with one final thrust and pour into him. I'm not just ejaculating, I'm letting go of everything I've held inside. I'm giving him everything I am, and everything I want to be. I roll to my side, but don't pull out of him. I'm not ready to let him go.

"Are you okay?" Please be okay.

"More than okay. Is it always like that? I've been missing out on so much."

"No, baby. It's not always like that." It's never like that. At least not in my experience. "That was special. You're special."

"Maybe *we're* special."

One of us should be panicking right now. Not two minutes ago, I told him I would pull out and I didn't. I so didn't.

He looks well and truly fucked, but happy. And I'm fucking smiling. I'm...happy too.

CHAPTER TWELVE

BECKETT

It's been three days since our first time and I'm sore. Really sore. But I seem to forget that every time I see that hungry look in his eyes. Which is a lot. He's a man with an appetite.

We're snuggled on the couch, my back to his front.

His gigantic hand is rubbing circles on my belly, and it feels better than nice. He wasn't lying when he said he liked my stomach. He never shies away from stroking me there.

"Beckett..."

I tilt my head back and look at him upside down. "You're insatiable. I need at least fifteen more minutes and maybe some food first."

"Ha-ha." He leans forward and kisses my forehead. "We need to talk." I freeze in a terribly stereotypical male move, so I sit up and turn to him.

"Relax, will ya?"

"It's never a good thing when someone says those words."

He shoves my shoulder. "How would you know? Neither of us have been in a relationship before. But don't worry, I'm not going to ask you about feelings or anything."

"Are you going to ask me to suck your dick again. The answer is yes." His eyes darken, and I can see where his mind goes as if a movie of us is playing on his forehead. "I love the way you taste."

He gets thoughtful, like he's looking into the future. "I'm rethinking living on an oil rig."

"You want your condo back?"

Okay, this conversation is not going the way I thought it would. My face must be showing my confusion because he mirrors it back to me.

"No."

"You mean, live together permanently?"

"You sound surprised."

"It's just," I begin. "Well, we're only three days into a sexual relationship, and I didn't think we were there yet."

"I see."

Have I hurt his feelings? "For a guy who told me he's never dated, just fucked men, I'm not sure how to read your reaction, Matthew."

He links his hands behind his head and leans back, staring at the ceiling. "We're more than 'three days into a *sexual relationship*.' I told you I love you."

"That doesn't mean you're ready to live with me."

"What if I am? Besides, I already am."

This is crazy. It doesn't make sense. "As roommates. This is differ—"

I'm on my back before I can finish the sentence. He grinds into me, knowing how easy I get ready for him. "Yeah, it's fast. Yeah, it's fucking nuts. But I love you. I want it all with you. I don't want to wait or put things off. If I learned anything from Cameron, it's that time isn't guaranteed." He grinds his hips again. "If you're not ready, we can wait. But I'm all in."

"Matthew...living together would change everything."

"So, let's change everything. Let's get married."

"Married? Are you serious?"

He reaches between us, but it's not to undo his pants like I think. He's in his pocket, and he's pulling out a ring. "Serious as fuck."

I'm staring at the pewter band in shock when the doorbell chimes. I start to get up, but he pushes me back down. "I'll get it. You look like you're about to pass out." He kisses me hard on my mouth and pushes off the couch.

I *am* about to pass out. I can't process anything. When did he buy the ring? We went out for a bit yesterday. To the mall he says he hates. He had to be pretty sneaky, though.

He answers the door to two of our neighbor kids dressed in their uniforms selling cookies. I get up to join him as he crouches down low and talks to young Etta, who will be in my class this fall. Her mom looks like her ovaries might be exploding like fireworks at the sight of my man with her small child, and I don't blame her.

He looks good with children. Really good. And of course, Etta is wrapping him around her finger talking about camp and cookies and how she lost her tooth yesterday.

"Becks, will you bring my checkbook? It's on my dresser."

"Only if you order the peanut butter ones."

He flashes me a grin over his shoulder. He's just amazing when he smiles.

I go into his room, a place he hasn't slept in for three days, and find there are two checkbooks on his dresser. Maybe he has a savings account or something. The first one I open says *Prime Trust Account* at the top, so I put it back and get the other, which is a personal checking account.

I get about four steps out of his room when it hits me.

Prime Trust was the name of my scholarship. Why would he have their checking account? I'm still frowning while he writes the check and brings the cookies into the kitchen.

"Where were we?" he asks. Then gets down on one knee and pulls out that ring. "Beckett, will you marry me?"

My mind is racing a million miles an hour. The bank account. The ring. It's too much. All of it together.

I look at him and his face is earnest. He thinks he's in love. He really believes it.

But I know better.

"No."

CHAPTER THIRTEEN

MATTHEW

I guess I should have been prepared. But I wasn't.

All the blood leaves my head, and I want to die. He's smart and he's right. He should hold off for someone who can give him more...you know what? Fuck that.

I will give him everything. Every damn thing.

He loves me. I know he does. And he might be smart, but he's got blinders on if he thinks this kind of love comes around more than once.

"You haven't been honest with me." He's pale and shaking, so I pull him down to the floor with me.

"What are you talking about?"

"When you sent me into your room, you forgot there were two checkbooks. One I brought to you. The other..."

Shit. "Prime Trust."

He raises his accusing eyes to mine. "Well?"

"It's not what you think." I have no idea what he's thinking. It's probably exactly what he thinks.

"Tell me what it is then."

"It's not a big deal."

"Really? I think it's a pretty big deal. Either you paid for my entire college education, including room and board. Or you have somehow stolen the checkbook of a trust account and are forging checks. Something tells me it's the first one."

"I was going to tell you."

"When?" He draws his legs up like he did on the couch the other day when he was closing up on himself. "So, I'm your charity case."

"What? No."

"You paid for my education. You won't take rent for the condo." His eyes widen. "Oh my God. The condo? You never even lived here. You got it for me, didn't you?" He slaps a palm over his forehead. "And the car. What else? Were you personally lining up all my dates for me? And when I couldn't close a deal, you stepped in and took one for the team? I'm so stupid. I thought..."

"You're not stupid. I've been taking care of you, yeah. But everything between us is real."

"Real? Are you joking right now? How can it be real if you were never honest with me? Did you get me my job, too?"

I shake my head. "No, baby. I swear. That's all you. I was just trying to help. Trying to do what Cam asked. Take care of you."

He hunches over like I just hit him in the stomach. Fuck. I am bad at this. "Cameron? This is all about Cameron?" He starts rocking. "I knew it was too good to be true. You know, after he died...everything was so bad. But then things started going my way. I thought maybe he was an angel looking out for me. The scholarship, God, that was everything. I didn't have to worry about anything for four years. When I won that car...when you asked me to housesit? I should have known. The only honest thing in my life has been that no man wants to be with me. But you swooped right in to fix that, too. Didn't you?"

"It's not like that and you know it."

I put my hand on his shoulder, but he shivers away from my touch. Like I'm going to hurt him. Fuck.

"What I know, Matthew, is that nothing in my life is real."

"I'm real. I swear to God, Becks. I'm real." I stop myself from reaching for him again. "You're pissed and I get that. I should have told you a long time ago about the scholarship. Cameron…he was my best friend. He loved you and your parents so much. He asked me to look out for you—and I knew I had nothing to offer but money. So I made sure you got it without ever feeling like you owed me anything. It was all for Cameron."

"You think Cameron wanted you to fuck me?"

Now I recoil like he sucker-punched me. And he did.

"No. No, I think he would make sure nobody ever found my body. I'm not good enough for you. I know that. Cam sure as hell would have known that. I never meant to fall for you."

He rolls his eyes. "Right. Because I am just impossible to resist. God. It would have been kinder for you to just tell me why no one wanted to go out with me twice. What you did…making me feel things that weren't true. Making me feel sexy and wanted…that was cruel."

"Beckett, you are sexy. So fucking sexy. And I hate that I hurt you. I knew I would screw this up. Hurt you. I never meant to. When you asked me to teach you…"

"Oh, God. I am so lame." His hands cover his face. Hiding from me.

"You are so perfect. You are everything to me." I want to touch him so bad. Wipe away all the doubts.

"Beckett, look at me."

He shakes his head.

"C'mon, baby. Look at me."

His hands lower. "Don't call me baby."

"I bought you a ring yesterday. Do you think I would do that just to help you get a second date with someone?"

"You have bought my entire life for five years. So, yes. It's extremely likely that you have some misplaced guilt or feelings of debt to my brother and were willing to sacrifice your future to make sure you honored your promise to him to take care of me. In fact, once you slept with me, you probably felt like you had to marry me in case I got pregnant. To appease Cam."

"You think I faked everything the last few days?"

"I don't want to. But how can I trust anything you say when you've been hiding huge secrets from me? I don't want you to feel like you have to take care of me. I want to be your equal. Your partner. Not a promise to my brother. Not a burden."

I can't believe I never thought of how he might feel finding out this way. "You're not a burden. I swear. Since the moment I stepped foot in this condo, I've been in love with you. I tried to fight it. I didn't think I was good enough for you. I still don't. And I will always take care of you. That's not going to change. Whether you're my husband or the man who won't speak to me that I just have to fucking love from afar like some idiot from one of those romantic movies you like so much. Beckett, you are mine, and I am yours, and that will never change."

"I can't do this. I'm sorry."

"Please don't tell me this is over. I can't...please don't." It figures that the one damn time I ever wanted anything, I was going to lose it.

"I'm going to go stay with Jenn while I look for a new place to live."

Inside my head, I am screaming, but I keep a lid on it and try to keep calm. "You don't have to do that. Stay here. I'll go. You stay."

"It's your condo. I need...I need to figure out how to build a life without my guardian angel paying all my bills. I know you were doing what you thought was best for me, and that you didn't mean to hurt me. But I'd never have let you do all this for me if I'd known. And I think you knew that or you would have been honest from the beginning. It's not just that I feel in your debt, Matthew, though I do. The other problem is that you think it's in your rights to lie to me to get the desired achievement. And that's not okay. Despite your heart being in the right place, it's not okay for you to take away my choices or protect me from the truth." He pauses. "You need to let me go."

"I don't think I can do that."

"You need to figure out how. And I need to learn how to stand on my own, without your help."

He's already made up his mind. The shell-shocked gaze is gone, and in its place, a quiet determined look. "Will you give me a chance? Please, Beckett."

"I don't ever see us being together. Not really."

My heart cracks like he's wielding a sledgehammer instead of a steely reserve.

I know I need to let him go. I won't give up. But I understand what he's saying. He's independent, and I have been keeping him in a cage without even telling him.

I honestly don't know how to go back to the guy I was even a month ago.

I guess I taught him how to break me after all.

CHAPTER FOURTEEN

BECKETT, TWO MONTHS LATER

I switch the phone to my other ear and Jenn is still chattering. "Come out with us," she says.

Not a chance.

"I'm tired."

"You're always tired. We'll go to that bear bar you were talking about."

Not. Even. Tempted. Though seeing Jenn and her boyfriend in a gay bar might be fun some other day. "Those kids wear me out. You hang out with five-year-olds all day and then tell me you want to go hang out in a bar with men who are even more immature than the kids were."

I have a busy night planned. Pizza. Chocolate. Bridget Jones. I don't even care if that makes me sound stereotypically gay. Tonight, I intend to be a flaming homo and the world can just suck it.

If I can manage to keep anything down that is. I rub my stomach. I have a little problem growing inside. Though I have a hard time calling it a problem. Except when I'm bent over the toilet.

Jenn sighs. "None of the men are ever going to compare to Matthew for you. You should just call him."

I look around my tiny apartment. It's a studio on top of someone's garage, but it's within walking distance of the school. Which is good because I sold my car to start paying

Matthew back. "I can't call him." He's probably back on the rig anyway.

I wonder what he's going to do with the condo now. Will he rent it out? Will he even keep it? It's not my business, and I shouldn't care.

But I do and I always will.

My apartment is just right for me now, though. I got what little furniture I have from thrift stores, but I love every piece.

I just don't know how long this place will be big enough for two.

"Go have fun, Jenn. I'm really fine here. I don't want to go out, and I'm not secretly hoping you'll cajole me into changing my mind."

"Okay. But what if I cajole you into calling Matthew?"

I crumple a piece of paper near the mic on my phone. "What's that? Are you going through a tunnel? You're breaking up."

"Ha-ha. Fine. But brunch tomorrow."

"Absolutely. Have fun."

It occurs to me, while watching Renee Zellweger singing alone in her apartment, that I am…becoming pathetic. I'm only twenty-three. I have one three-day relationship and a string of bad first dates under my belt. It's too soon to give up. But the thought of anyone else touching me. No. Just no.

The thought of Matthew touching me. Well, that's better.

But anyway, who would want to date me now? I'll be having another man's baby in seven months.

What would I do if Mathew knocked on my door right now? I pause the movie and lean back, closing my eyes. I am, pathetically, wearing his sweatshirt. It ended up in my laundry somehow, and I never returned it. Tonight, it was staring at me from the drawer, wondering why I never wear it, and I figured, what the hell? It doesn't smell like him anymore, but it's comforting anyway.

I imagine Matthew and...I hear a knock at the door?

Fucking Jenn. She is wasting both our time. I do not want to go out tonight.

I swing the door open. "Go away! I've got a man in here," I joke.

"Uh, bad time?"

I imagine my eyes are cartoonishly round as I stare at Matthew. Matthew!

"Wh-what are you doing here?"

He starts to answer then stops, taking in my appearance. I can see when he realizes I'm wearing his shirt. Shit.

He swallows hard. "I've interrupted." His brow furrows into wrinkles of pain. "I'm sorry. Here's your mail." He thrusts two envelopes into my hand and turns to go.

I think about letting him leave believing there is another man here. But I call out, "Matthew, wait."

He stops at the bottom of the stairs and looks up. God, the stricken expression on his face guts me. "Please come up. You're not interrupting anything. There's nobody here. I thought you were Jenn."

Eyebrows raised, he stalks back up the stairs slowly. God, he looks amazing. This is the first time I've seen him since I moved out. He's better than the mental pictures my memory served up.

A hot flush steals over me as he gets closer. All that towering strength. All those corded, bunching muscles. I swallow hard and try to still my heart. It's thumping so hard he can probably see it.

And I'm already hard.

He stops in front of me on the landing. "You smell good, Beckett."

I hold it together for another second or two while we stare into each other's eyes. And then I throw myself into his arms.

He sweeps me into his embrace and brings me into the house.

"This is a bad idea," I protest, but I nestle my face into his neck. He doesn't smell like cookies, but oh my God, does he smell amazing. He doesn't wear cologne—it's the scent of his soap and shampoo and just him. Just him.

He settles us onto the little lumpy couch with me on his lap and squeezes me, rubbing small circles on my back. I pull back to look at him. "I need to tell you something."

"Anything."

I almost let it out, say the words. He's here, he's really here. And he wants me. I can feel how much underneath my ass. But, I need to know he's not only here out of misplaced responsibility. He'd marry me for sure if he knew I was pregnant. I need to know this is real. That he's not just keeping a promise to a dead man. "I...I just miss you."

"I miss you, too. God, Becks. More than you know." He cups my cheek. "I've been going crazy."

"Me, too."

Matthew kisses my forehead. I can feel his arousal beneath me. He's hard and ready to take me. All that's standing between us is my stupid pride.

ROOMMATES

I swallow hard. Swallow the ball of pride that's made me miserable for two months. Yes, I can do it. I can take care of myself. I can pay my bills and get along day to day. But it's half a life. It's certainly not the life I want.

His hand squeezes my leg and a guttural groan escapes him. "Becks."

"I don't want to dream about you anymore."

CHAPTER FIFTEEN

MATTHEW

I'm on the edge of a cliff, and I'm afraid to breathe.

He's here. He's with me. I'm finally touching my man again, and for the first time in my life, I am fucking scared.

He shifts, and I'm afraid he's going to get up and kick me out. Instead, he straddles me, right where I need him most. "You have to be honest with me. From now on. If I can ever learn to trust in you...in myself...again...you can't keep things from me."

Something that feels like sunshine lights up inside my chest. Is he going to give me another chance? "Baby, whatever you want. I promise."

"I don't ever want to feel like that again. I don't want to wonder if you're just acting or doing something because you think it's the honorable thing to do. I want you to want me. Just me."

I open my palm, and he gasps. "Put this fucking ring on and you will never, ever doubt me again. I promise."

He lets out a watery laugh. "That's a pretty romantic proposal."

"You never said you wanted romance."

"You've been holding that since you got here?"

I nod. God. If this doesn't work. I don't think I can go back to a world without him in it. "I know I don't deserve you. If Cam were here..."

"If Cam were here, he would kick your ass. And then he would give you a beer and tell you all the ways you aren't allowed to screw up with me. And then he would give you his blessing because he loved you, Matthew."

"I'm not on the rig anymore. They transferred me to an office job. I kept the condo, but if you'd rather live in a house or a treehouse or a cave, you just tell me and we'll move." I look around. "Maybe not here, though."

He laughs. "You do look a little ridiculous here. I think you're bigger than my couch."

"Put on the fucking ring." I clear my throat. "Please."

"You can be a little domineering, you know."

"A little?" I take his hand and put the ring on it myself. It looks real good. I feel like I can breathe again when he doesn't tear it off. "You like it when I'm domineering." I'm going to remember this moment for the rest of my life. "You like it when I tell you what to do."

"In bed, yes. Try it anywhere else, I dare you."

Adrenaline rushes through me like I've just walked away from an explosion and my hands start to shake. "I came so close to losing you. I don't think I'm man enough to go through that ever again."

I squeeze him hard. Probably too hard. His ass fits into my hands like it was made to be there. He arches into my hold on him. Mine. He's mine.

"We don't have to go fast. If you want to wait, I get it. I rushed us last time. I mean, I don't expect you to have sex with me tonight. We can. I just don't want you to think I expect it."

Jesus. I sound like a real idiot.

"I don't want to go slow." He rolls his groin over my erection. "I feel like my life has been on hold until right now. I want it all. I'm ready if you are."

"Babe, I need to fuck you." I won't feel right again until I do. Until I'm deep inside him. I can't think straight now. I squeeze his plump ass and groan. "Right now."

He's undoing my jeans and we maneuver enough to get them down to my ankles while we pull down his pants. He grinds on me, the friction of us together feels good. But not as good as the vise of his ass is going to feel.

He pauses. "I have to tell you something."

Since he already said that a few minutes ago, I wonder what is on his mind.

"Anything, Beck. Anything at all."

His face gets green. "Oh no!" He claps a hand over his mouth and lurches off my lap.

"Baby, you okay?" I ask his back as he runs into the bathroom, slams the door, and starts retching.

Well, that figures. I finally get him back and he's got a stomach bug. At least I hope that's what it is and it wasn't the thought of having sex with him and made him sick.

I pull my pants up and go into his kitchen and find the cupboard with the tea he likes and fill the kettle with water. When he comes out of the bathroom, I've got his tea ready and a plate of crackers in case he thinks that will settle his stomach.

"Sorry about that," he says sheepishly.

"You don't have to apologize. Are you feeling better? We don't have to do anything tonight. I'd like to stay and take care of you though." I lead him back to his couch and hand him the cup. "Is it a virus or do you think it's food poisoning?"

He shakes his head me, but eagerly sips the tea. "No."

"What is going on then...wait a minute."

He stares at the mug in his hands, not looking at me.

"You're pregnant? Why didn't you say something sooner? How long have you known?"

"I went to the doctor yesterday. And I thought you were on the oil rig."

A baby. Whoa. "Are you okay? What did the doctor say?"

"Are you mad?"

"Mad? Why would I be mad? You're wearing my ring and having my baby. This is the best damned day of my life so far."

"Really?"

Yeah. My priorities sure have changed in the last few months. I never thought I wanted a husband, much less a pregnant one. And now life seems limitless. "I'm the happiest mother fucker on the planet right now."

He laughs at my garbage mouth.

"I love you so much, Matthew."

"I love you too, Beckett. And I promise to show you every day for the rest of our lives."

While I'd love to fuck him until sunrise, he looks pale and shaky, so we go to bed, spooning while my mind races and he snores lightly.

A father. Me. Holy shit. I don't know anything about pregnant omegas or childbirth or raising kids. Luckily, my partner will be a natural at all of it, but this probably won't be my first sleepless night in the next few months. Years.

I doze a bit in the early morning light and wake up to his mouth waking up my dick.

"Damn, Becks. That's the best way to wake up."

He lifts his head and smiles at me, lighting up the room more than the noon sun ever could. He slides up my body and we make out like teenagers for what seems like hours. Until I'm ready to explode.

We use old fashioned spit and my leaking pre-cum as lube. Beckett slides down my pole slowly, and we both groan. When he's seated all the way, when my balls are touching his ass, he starts undulating those hips in slow circles, riding me, grinding me. He's stretched tight around my girth, and I bite my lip to keep myself from ramming hard. The air is sawing in and out of me like I want my cock in him to be doing.

Nothing has ever felt like this before. Not even our first time. Because there are no secrets between us now. I'm not behind the scenes controlling his life. He chose me. He can survive without me, but he doesn't want to.

He leans over and flicks one of my nipples with his tongue, and my hips arch off the bed. "Becks," I warn.

Then he bites it.

"Fuck," I roar, digging my fingers into his hips, I let go of my restraint.

I'm fucking him hard and he's taking it, making this sweet moaning sound I feel in my bones. He tilts his head back and holds on to me like he's riding a bull. And I start milking his cock, loving the smooth velvet slide.

And then he surrenders, covering my hand in his sweet cum. He's pulling me deeper inside, milking me. The rhythm is so beautiful and wild. I can't stop myself from joining him, filling him up with the essence of who I am and what I was made to do.

He's mine. I smooth my thumb down the column of his throat and feel his erratic pulse there. His eyes fly open and a secret smile graces his handsome face.

"I love you, Beckett. I swear you'll never doubt that another day of your life. I know I suck at relationship stuff. But I'll spend the rest of my life trying to get better."

"I love you, Matthew. And I don't think you suck as bad as you think you do."

He rolls his hips and I start to harden again. "You think I can get through this whole day without pulling out of you once?"

"I've always appreciated a good challenge," he says. And we spend our first day as an engaged couple naked from sunup to sundown.

CHAPTER SIXTEEN

BECKETT, TWO MONTHS LATER

My new husband is looking down at me through half-lidded lashes, giving me that dirty smile I love as I run a hand through the thick pelt of fur between his pecs with one hand and pinch one of his small, perfect nipples with the other.

He grunts as the nipple beads up, and he delves a hand through my hair, grasping as much as he can in his big, callused paw. I suck on the nipple, rolling it in my mouth, nipping it with my teeth the way that makes him crazy, then transfer to the other to give it the same treatment. It's our wedding night and he promised me I could play as long as I wanted to on the wonderland that is his body. Usually, I only get a few minutes of foreplay before he gets impatient. He can play with *me* for hours, but if I try to dawdle with him, he can't take it.

Which is why he's sitting in the chair and I'm standing, leaning over his body.

He drags my hand roughly to his cock. It's huge already, pushing hard against the zipper of his tux pants.

"Don't rush me," I say, pulling my hand back.

He exhales a low, "Fuck," and I go back to mapping his upper body with my tongue. I love his broad chest, the dense powerful muscles beneath that honey-bronzed skin.

"Fuck, fuck, fuck," he carries on in whisper-groans.

I take pity on my husband...my husband...I'll never get tired of saying that...and massage the beast in his pants. I get on my knees and press my face into his crotch and nuzzle, making sure he's making eye contact with me while I do because that seems to drive him over the edge most times. And I want him to remember this night forever.

I can't believe we're married.

"Please, baby. Take it out."

I smile at his manners. In another five minutes, he'll be all caveman on me. There will be no please or thank you then. At least not until we both come.

I unzip him slowly, with my teeth of course, and his cock pops out of his boxer briefs and hits me in the cheek, dabbing my skin with pre-cum.

He grunts a rumble of pleasure again. "My cock looks good on your face."

Kissing the side of his shaft makes his hips surge up. "Your cock looks good anywhere. It's a beautiful thing."

His legs are splayed wide and I squeeze him, hard like he likes it. He's not one for gentle caresses.

"Jesus Christ, if you want this to last, you need to stop being so good at this. I'm going to come in your hand, baby."

I lick the salty slit of his crown before I say, "That's okay. I'm going to drain you many, many times tonight."

He yanks me up with one powerful arm and thrusts his tongue in my mouth. Our teeth scrape and gnash, our stubbled cheeks and chins scrape against each other. He tongue fucks my mouth until I'm panting like a dog in summer, and then he pushes me back down his barbarian's body until I'm face to face with his dick.

I'm past finesse as I slurp him up, taking him in as far as I can. I love the weight of him in my mouth. I love the musky scent of him. I just want to worship his cock. Deeper and deeper I take him until his pubes are brushing against my face.

I have gotten really good at this the last few months. Must be that I enjoy my practicing so much.

"I can't..." Matthew doesn't finish his thought. Instead, he groans and his cock swells in my mouth and begins to pulse, surging as he shoots his cum right down my throat.

Stars burst behind my eyelids, but I don't pull off until he slumps back into the chair. I crawl into his lap as we catch our breath.

"Baby, why did you make me come so fast?" He kisses my hair. "It's our wedding night. I wanted to last longer."

I'm still hard as granite. "We're not done."

We finish undressing all the way and land on the bed in a heap. Matthew reaches for the bottle and hands it to me.

"Are you sure?" I ask.

We saved one first for tonight. His first and mine.

"I've been dying to feel you inside me, Becks."

I'm going to fuck my man.

He's never trusted anyone before me. And we've almost done it plenty of times, but then he decided he thought it would be quaint, his word, to be a virgin on his wedding night.

"Roll over, you beast." Once he's settled, I straddle him, my cock resting at the top of his ass. God, it looks amazing there. I can't help but rub between his cheeks some. I use the lotion to oil up his strong back, massaging him slowly up and down until he is bonelessly relaxed beneath me. But I'm so hard it hurts.

I move down, straddling his legs now, and massage his butt. He's got buns of steel, and I grab the globes and pull them apart so I can rim him out with my tongue. He's extremely sensitive there and his whole-body jerks.

"Okay?" I ask

"Fuck, yeah. That feels great."

"Get on your knees, Matthew. All fours. I want to ride you."

I love it when he dominates me, but sometimes, I like to turn the tables. He does what I say and I oil my dick up. I have to squeeze the tip so I don't come now.

God, his big hulking body is stupid sexy. I can't believe I'm so lucky. I can't believe it every day when I get to wake up next to him. When he tells me he loves me. And now, I'm going to get me a piece of ass.

My cock is not as big as his, but it is not small. I don't want to hurt him. I used the crown to tease his sensitive nerves around the rim, and he starts rocking involuntarily.

"Fuck me, Beckett."

I push in, past the tight ring, and we both groan as it twitches around me. "Okay, honey?" I ask.

"Oh, fuck yeah." Before I can ease in further, he pushes all the way back and impales himself on me. It knocks the breath out of him for a second, his legs start shaking. I hold on and hold still.

God, he feels fantastic. "You're so tight. You're squeezing me. Feels so good."

He grunts and I start fucking my husband with slow, steady thrusts.

"That curve on your dick is hitting me just right, Beckett." He gasps and squeezes the sheets.

I am glad to hear it as I grasp his oiled body and just start rutting. I can't even help it. I'm just unable to control my hips any longer. We're sweaty and slick from the lube. He's bucking and I'm thrusting and riding him.

The bed is creaking. This might end up being an expensive hotel stay if we bust it, but all I care about is plowing him deeper. I'm close, really close.

I lean forward and bite his back, probing him hard with my cock, and grasping his dick in my hand. "Come, Matthew," I demand.

He pours into my hand, roaring loud enough to get us kicked out of the honeymoon suite for sure. But I let go and fill him until we collapse on the bed and practically pass out.

After napping, showering, and eating room service, we're snuggled on the couch in matching robes and I start laughing.

"What?" he asks. "What's so funny over there."

"I'm just trying to imagine how I would have reacted if someone had told me a few months that this night was possible. I can't believe I ever thought you were straight."

"I've never even kissed a woman. You?"

It's weird we've never talked about it. We've been lucky, I guess, in that we don't have horror coming out stories, either.

I nod. "Prom date. It wasn't like 'recoil in horror' or anything. She was a nice girl. But it did nothing for me. I told her I respected her too much to go any further." He hasn't replied, but he's tense behind me. "Do not tell me you are jealous right now. You asked."

"I know. I'm big and stupid. Some things I don't want to know." He kisses my head. "Tell me we never have to speak of this again," he says, holding me tighter.

"We never have to speak of this again."

He blows out a long sigh. "I love you."

"I love you, too." I hold up our entwined hands, then place them on my belly where the baby has just woken up. "I won't be able to do what we did in a few weeks. My stomach is getting bigger every day."

He rubs circles in the circle of hair there and then splays his hand over our baby bump protectively. "I've always loved your stomach. I love it even more now."

"Well, that's good. There's a whole lot more to love lately."

"It's amazing to me that you can grow a whole person inside you. And I like it even more now that you're showing."

"I like it that I'm not throwing up all the time."

"That too."

He gets quiet. Too quiet. That's his thinking too hard quiet. I sit up. "What's wrong?"

"I'm just wondering what kind of dad I'll be. I didn't have one to look up to. I never thought I'd even ever think about it."

I cup his cheek. "You're going to be an awesome dad. You're a good man, Matthew. I wouldn't have shackled myself to you for life if I didn't think so."

He nods, but he's still worried. "I just don't ever want to disappoint you."

This is heavier talk than I anticipated for our wedding night. "Babe, you're my hero. You could never disappoint me."

He smiles and his cheeks get pink for second before he recovers. "You just want to see me in tights and that ain't happening."

I untie his robe. "How about a cape…and nothing else?"

"When did you become so insatiable?"

"The first time you kissed me."

That was the right answer judging by the look in his eye. "You're being very naughty. I'm going to have to teach you a lesson."

I can't wait for my private lessons to resume.

CHAPTER SEVENTEEN

MATTHEW, FIVE MONTHS LATER

He's baking again. It's a little odd, but my husband has spent the last two weeks baking, cleaning up after baking, or freezing what he baked. When he relaxes, he's looking at Pinterest for different things to bake next.

"Babe, the second freezer is almost full. We're going to have to hit the appliance store for a third freezer today if you don't stop making cookies."

"It's bread today." He rubs his lower back. "I'm nesting."

I kiss the top of his head and reach around to massage the sore muscles for him. "Are you okay? You seem off today."

And pale. With dark blue thumbprints under his eyes. Frankly, he looks like shit, but I'm not about to tell him that.

"I didn't sleep well last night."

"Maybe you should take a break from baking and put your feet up for a while. Maybe take a nap."

"I've thought about it. But then I keep baking. I thought nesting would be cleaning. At least we'll have bread in the freezer when we have a newborn."

He slumps into my embrace and a fresh rush of love overwhelms me. I can't explain how I continue to fall in love with my husband more every day. My life is unrecognizable from a year ago, and it just keeps getting better. And soon, we'll have a daughter. That just blows me away.

He stiffens like he's in pain. "My back is really spasming a lot today. Maybe I should go put my feet up."

"Do you want a hot bath? I can get the tub ready for you."

"Oh, that would be nice. Thank..." He gasps. "Oh my God."

His voice alarms me. "What is it?"

He pulls away from me and stares down at his legs. "My water just broke."

"Are you serious?" I look down at his wet jeans. "Holy shit. Your water just broke."

"What do we do?" he asks me.

It's not often he is at a loss. It's not like we haven't been over the scenario a billion times. But he looks scared and every instinct in me wants to make him feel safe again. "You go sit. I'll get the bags and call the doctor. Then I'll drive us to the hospital and pretty soon, we'll have our little girl."

"The C-Section is scheduled for next week. She can't come today." He squeezes my hand. "I'm not ready. She needs to wait."

I pull him into a hug. "You're ready. You're going to be such a great dad. I can't wait to meet our little Darcy."

Hearing her name, the name we agreed on to remember the night everything seemed to change, makes him relax. "Okay. Yes. We can do this."

I'm doing a good job of hiding my nerves. I know I need to be strong for Beckett, but frankly, I'm scared as fuck. I know birthing a baby is painful and dangerous. I'm excited to finally hold our baby, but I hate that my husband's health is risked to bring her here.

They're ready for us when we arrive, and then it's all fast and furious. Someone is helping me into scrubs, telling me things I'm only half listening to as I watch them prep my husband, tenting his abdomen and putting a mask over his nose. I feel better, marginally, when I get to stand next to him.

As big and tough as I am, I catch a glimpse of the surgery in the mirror above us and almost pass out.

But I have to be strong. Beckett and Darcy need me.

Then it's over and they wheel his table out and take me with Darcy to get weighed and cleaned up. I promised Becks I wouldn't leave her side until we were all together again, but the alpha in me does not like that they took my husband out of my sight. I only feel complete when we're together.

And then I look at the baby, really look at her. And I fall in love for the second time in my life.

Epilogue

BECKETT
Two Years Later

I'm standing in front of the window of the wine storee and it's now or never.

Beetlejuice, better known as Darcy, our two-year-old, is snoozing in her stroller. I could never bring her in there when she's awake. She's an escape artist, and it's because of her that I can't have nice things.

Except that she's the best, nicest thing that ever happened to her daddy and me.

I push the stroller into the store and try to take in everything at once. I don't know how long my window of opportunity is before the little monster wakes up, so I need to shop fast if I want to surprise Matthew.

A slender woman approaches and then we both smile when we recognize each other. Leslie from the lingerie shop. She gives me a hug and tells me my baby looks sweet.

"All babies look sweet when they're asleep," I tell her.

"Are you okay? You look a little..." She's searching for a word that means tired and worn-out, but one that wouldn't offend me.

"I'm exhausted. You can say it."

Leslie tsked. "Seems like Matthew is the kind of guy who would help you out more."

"How do you know I ended up with Matthew?" I ask.

She picks up my left hand. "I helped him pick out this ring to surprise you."

What? "The day we were at the mall together?"

She nods. "Yeah, he called me. Asked me to pick out five rings and I sent him pictures from my phone. My friend at the jeweler across the way held them, and two days later he ran down here while you were in the bathroom to buy it."

"Wow. I had no idea. I remember wondering how he'd managed to get it." My heart blooms and my face heats.

"Still a blushing groom, I see."

"He takes good care of me still. Of us. It's not his fault I'm tired." I pause. "Actually, it is his fault. I'm telling him tonight that I'm pregnant again. I heard this shop has a good selection of non-alcoholic wine."

Leslie is even better with wine than she was with lingerie, and when Darcy wakes up, we're already halfway to the car.

I just hope that Matthew is okay with this. We haven't talked about having another baby—this one is more than a handful and runs us both ragged. I know he'll love another child—but will he be excited about one?

MATTHEW

I take a quick, hot shower after finally getting the baby to sleep. I don't know how my husband handles her alone all day long. He says he wants to be a stay-at-home dad for now, but man, Darcy has to be more work than a classroom full of kindergarteners.

I come out of the bathroom to find my husband passed out. Can't blame him really.

I get him tucked in, removing all the decorative pillows he insists we need on the bed every day, when I see what looks like a flat pen tucked under one.

Holy shit. It's a pregnancy test.

I'm sure he meant to present it to me while...conscious. But I can't wait until morning, so I look.

It's positive.

Holy shit.

Is he happy? Excited? Resigned? I don't want to wake him up since he obviously needs all the sleep he can get.

Am I happy?

His last pregnancy crosses my mind. The way he waddled. His cravings. The feel of the baby kicking my hand. Holding Darcy for the first time.

Yeah. Yeah, I'm fucking stoked.

I can't believe I'm the same guy who didn't want a family. Or a husband. Or even a home. My family is everything to me now. Life is crazy most of the time. But it's good crazy. It's damn good crazy.

My childhood was a mess—but that just means I try harder. Give my kid the stability I never had. Give my husband the love my mom was always looking for but was too drugged out to ever find.

I spoon around my spouse and put my hand on his belly where our baby grows.

"I'll keep my promise, Cameron," I whisper, in case he's listening. "I'll take care of your baby brother until my last breath."

Don't miss out!

Visit the website below and you can sign up to receive emails whenever Briton Frost publishes a new book. There's no charge and no obligation.

https://books2read.com/r/B-A-VDMG-GOHX

BOOKS 2 READ

Connecting independent readers to independent writers.

Did you love *Roommates*? Then you should read *Forget Me Knot: An Mpreg Romance* by Briton Frost!

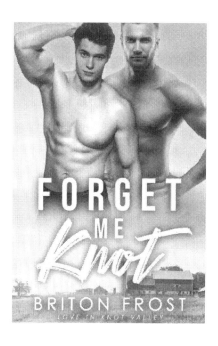

After serving five years of a ten-year sentence for a crime he didn't commit, coming home to Knot Valley after being vindicated should be alpha Luke Barker's triumph. All he wants is the life he was supposed to have—a thriving farm, a strong family, and a house full of kids. He should have learned by now that nothing is fair, and he'll have to work just as hard to make it on the outside as he did to survive in prison.

The fields are fallow, his house is falling down around his nearly catatonic father, and his ex-boyfriend is somebody else's husband now. But he's not giving up. He'll replant the crops, fix the house, and find an omega of his own. Not in that order, because a man has needs, and his have been denied too long.

Michael, the quirky omega waiter at the diner downtown, could use someone looking out for him, and Luke needs a favor in return. Starting with a baby.

This farmer is about to take a husband.

Welcome to Knot Valley, a sleepy small town in Eastern Washington. *Forget me Knot* **is the first in the series about super dominant alphas and quirky omegas finding love and creating families in an alternate universe where mpreg is possible. Some of the books are reimagined from a different series. If you like your MM steamy and endings happy, this hot series will get you right in the feels.**

Read more at https://www.britonfrost.com/.

Also by Briton Frost

Love in Knot Valley
Forget Me Knot: An Mpreg Romance
Sorry Knot Sorry: An Mpreg Romance
Ready or Knot: An Mpreg Romance
Thou Shall Knot: An Mpreg Romance
Knot Christmas Without You: An Mpreg Romance
All for Knot: An Mpreg Romance

Love in Knot Valley Series Collection
Love in Knot Valley: 1-3

Standalone
Roommates

Watch for more at https://www.britonfrost.com/.

About the Author

Briton Frost writes books in an alternate universe where men can impregnate each other. Some of the books are reimagined books from a different series because Briton can't stop playing the "what if?" game and doesn't want to let characters go without exploring them in different situations.

Visit Briton on Facebook: https://www.facebook.com/BritonFrost/

Read more at https://www.britonfrost.com/.

Printed in Great Britain
by Amazon